SUNBURST

Thelma Barrington's life was restricted to caring for her late parents. She feels old — like a maiden aunt — useful for babysitting and minding the family pet. When she's suddenly thrown together with Myron, a charming, younger man, he proposes marriage. This wonderful chance of a new life is shadowed by doubts: is it her bank balance that attracts him? And, when, following a tragedy, Thelma has to care for her two young nephews, will Myron stay — or just walk away?

MAVIS THOMAS

SUNBURST

Complete and Unabridged

LINFORD
Leicester

First published in Great Britain in 2011

First Linford Edition
published 2011

British Library CIP Data

Thomas, Mavis.
    Sunburst. - - (Linford romance library)
    1. Single women- -Family relationships- -
    Fiction. 2. Love stories. 3. Large type books.
    I. Title II. Series
    823.9'2–dc22

    ISBN 978–1–4448–0770–7

Published by
F. A. Thorpe (Publishing)
Anstey, Leicestershire

Set by Words & Graphics Ltd.
Anstey, Leicestershire
Printed and bound in Great Britain by
T. J. International Ltd., Padstow, Cornwall

This book is printed on acid-free paper

1

From the window of that big front bedroom you could see almost all of The Crescent. Today, through my sister Lesley's filmy curtains, I surveyed the road transformed and glorified. After a dragging winter and a tardy spring, at last the solid, unremarkable houses stood now mellowed and drowsy in early May sunshine. Gardens were breaking into life. Lines of ornamental cherry trees contrasted their wondrous pink with the blue sky.

So each year those trees touched our London suburb briefly with fairy dust. The Crescent hadn't changed. But we had known change — and soon would know more.

The shattering news I had just announced was still sinking into Lesley's mind. On the bed she sat dumfounded amid a chaos of abandoned packing.

She said just my name, 'Thelma!' And then, with all the dismay and disbelief I had expected, 'Is this some kind of joke? You're not serious? . . . are you?'

'It's not any kind of joke. I'll tell you again,' I said patiently. 'He asked me to marry him. Last night when all the others had gone. I said I'd think about it — and I've thought, and the answer is yes.'

Again I turned to the window, not wanting to see the worry and disquiet on her face. She mumbled, 'Look — you know I don't want to be unkind, but — surely you can see it *wouldn't* work out, not you and him! Just for starters, he'll want a lively, bubbly young wife, the sort he can take around and show off, not — '

'Not a miserable stick-in-the-mud he'll be ashamed of. Thanks a lot!'

'Thelma, that's not true. You've had a very hard time nursing poor Dad so long, you deserve some happiness if ever anyone did . . . but — oh, I did think you were too sensible to rush into marriage with the first man to ask you!'

I said somewhat tartly, 'Yes, he's the first. Thanks again for pointing it out.'

Looking back over the years, it did seem a little unfair that my two sisters — both Lesley and Janine happily married with flourishing families, both younger than myself — took it for granted I would live on in single blessedness as a convenient babysitter or pet-minder when needed. In this same house I had cared for our mother through her last illness, and after that came Dad's prolonged struggle against the disease that reduced him to a shadow of the man I remembered. He had relied on me utterly, and I vowed that while I could still care for him, no hospital ward should replace his own bed, his own kin.

When he died just before Christmas, we grieved for him deeply but couldn't wish his endurance prolonged. So he was laid to rest beside the wife who went ahead. People paused to pay their respects, and the tide of life swept on. And for me there came suddenly, almost unbelievably, a freedom strange and new.

I was around — vaguely around — my mid-thirties. I had inherited this roomy house in The Crescent, big enough for two families, which now Dad had left us and Lesley's family were vacating their upstairs flat, would be my solitary residence: and I had a fair sum in the bank that Dad had also left me. Though I felt guilty to inherit so much while just the rest of the money was shared between Lesley and Janine and their children, my sisters had no thought of unfairness. I had nursed our parents devotedly, they said. And they had their own homes, their own families, their own worlds.

'Of course, you'll let the top flat,' Lesley had cheerfully arranged my life for me. 'And you can get a job that interests you — like the one at the estate agents you had before Dad couldn't be left. And you must stay with

4

us or Jan for holidays and Christmas . . . '

So I was all wrapped up and disposed of. To the children I was 'Auntie Thelma', staid, strict, already nudging middle-age. To neighbours and acquaintances I was 'Miss Barrington', with respect and a marked reserve. It seemed I had always fitted into this role, even from childhood days, when Lesley and Jan had a lively circle of friends. They both resembled our mother, with a dark-haired, blue-eyed elfin charm. I took after Dad's side: almost five feet nine in bare feet, with undeniably the Barrington nose . . . and with grave grey eyes and my long fair hair coiled up formally. I was available for feeding people's menageries of pets, for fetching old Mrs. Bailey's shopping when she had another 'turn'. I was, at least, of use. Perhaps it didn't show that I was lonely.

Today, Lesley had so much more! She was even more attractive than in her quite gorgeous teens, even with her third child due very soon. Seven years ago she married quiet, kindly Martin

Percival — who, in a peak of irony, I had first met at a local Gardening Club. Any passing bitterness had long since faded, leaving just my sincere sisterly affection and respect for Martin. It was mainly down to him that the Percivals lingered so long in the upstairs flat, because he hadn't wanted me left alone during Dad's last stages.

Now they were moving out at last. I had visited the brand new house on a new Surrey estate and helped Lesley choose curtains and fittings — or stood by while she chose them. There was a big room for the small Percival sons, Phil and Richie, and another room awaiting the little girl Lesley so much wanted. Doubtless her wish would come true.

But before the move, she and Martin were travelling to Scotland for a short holiday with Janine. They were leaving today, hence the last minute packing I had just stopped dead in its tracks. Lesley wanted to make the visit before her baby arrived — for she had so much to discuss with Jan, who was expecting another baby too. Jan was the wife of Andrew Fraser, who she met on a Scottish holiday, and they had a nice house on the coast and a small daughter with a mass of her father's sandy-gold hair. For the next few days they would all have a wonderful time together . . .

'You know, you've really shaken me!' Lesley brought me abruptly back to the here and now. 'I always hoped you'd get married one day — '

'To someone suitable. Corpulent and bald, ready to retire and play endless golf. I'm getting just a bit tired of being labelled past my sell-by date.'

'Well, I'm sorry. But — does Gill know your age?'

'He realises I'm a bit older. That doesn't make me as old as the hills.'

'No. Certainly not. But — ' There seemed an endless supply of 'buts'. 'He's younger than Jan. You call her your kid sister.'

'Well? You'd take him for more.'

She seemed about to say you would

also take me for more, but thought better of it. She asked instead, 'Are you saying you're truly in love with him? Of course you're feeling flat and miserable after losing Dad — and the chance of a whole new life seems wonderful — but *think* about it, please *think*. You've scarcely known him three months — '

'I've spent lots of time with him.'

'Yes, doing all his behind-the-scenes political work, with other people around most of the time! He's turned you into his secretary and runabout and general dogsbody,' she insisted with some heat. 'He expects everyone to run round after him, then he takes all the credit and enjoys being Mr. Popular. Look at that sales promotion job at Hanley's . . .'

I sighed at yet another resurrection of that grievance.

It was a few months ago that Myron Gillespie made his first appearance at Hanley's Business Supplies, the London concern where Martin had worked long-time in his conscientious, unambitious way. Straight away the newcomer walked into a certain plum post, under the noses of Martin and various others with far more experience. Lesley had minded far more than Martin himself — especially because she believed 'that young upstart', as she called him, had captured the prize purely by an ability to make glittering promises, by radiating a plausible charm, by his own limitless self-confidence.

'Be honest, he does just trample roughshod over people,' she said now. 'Oh, he'll always be successful — he'll land himself a seat in Parliament somewhere as that's what he wants, and woe betide the workers who slave to do all the donkeywork! Yes, I can see it, you'll be the wife of a bright young go-ahead with his picture smiling at us all in the press and on the TV screens . . . and you'll work yourself to a shadow in the background! . . . '

When she paused for breath, it was quite hard to choke back an angry response. Of course, Lesley was prejudiced after the affair at Hanley's. Again I turned to the window, but not now to admire the cherry trees. There was a banner below in the front garden, and another opposite which Mrs. White, Lesley's close friend, had been persuaded to display:

'*MAKE MYRON GILLESPIE YOUR CHOICE! . . .* '

As far as the sphere of politics went, I had never been greatly interested: but some while back Dad joined the local branch of an organisation campaigning to cut down crime, protect the environment, aid the elderly, and various other laudable aims. Before he became housebound I went along to assist him to various meetings and discussion groups. Then I found myself drawn in to help at jumble sales and fêtes. They were friendly people, it made an interest outside the claustrophobic sickroom. And so I would probably have continued, an inconspicuous part of the background, had not a swift tide of events swept me along.

The local MP died, causing a by-election. Our candidate had just accepted a business opportunity in Canada. Martin happened to discuss it at work, and immediately Myron expressed a personal interest. In an incredibly short time he met the Constituency Committee and got on their short list. Soon I found myself bundling up leaflets bearing his name and a very striking photograph. I became what Lesley called darkly his 'dogsbody'.

And with Myron in the forefront, there were dramatic changes! We were sparked to new life, members no more than vague names on a list suddenly gave donations and distributed literature. With enthusiasm flaring, everyone had to do something . . . and my role was to turn my home into an office, spend hours phoning and emailing and typing — and lately to be at Myron's elbow at meetings, on doorsteps or platforms, arranging appointments, watching everyone succumb to his magical personality.

There were others he could have chosen to help him. He wanted me. To him I wasn't that detached 'Miss Barrington', I was 'Thelma', warmly and intimately. That magnetic smile in the most crowded room was only for me.

Perhaps Lesley didn't realise how I had long cherished a dream that one day I would share the warmth of fulfilment both my sisters already knew. Perhaps there was some truth in her idea that after years of willing restriction I was now too ready to surrender my natural caution. But had I not earned this belated freedom to live my own life, to love and be loved?

I looked across the road at those bold letters on the placard. For me their slogan held a very special and personal message.

* * *

It was as well there was no time to continue today's hurtful argument. A car had just drawn up outside, and I ran down to give and take some messages. When I returned, Richie was awake after his afternoon sleep.

'Mummy will be back very soon,' Lesley was reassuring him. 'And you'll have a lovely time here with Auntie Thelma, you'll see!'

'Tumming with *you*,' Richie said, unimpressed.

'But it's a long way, and you know you always feel bad travelling . . . and Auntie Thelma will buy you something nice! . . . '

He repeated, with tears overflowing, 'Don't want Auntie Felma. Don't *like* Auntie Felma. Tumming with *you*.'

Rather hopelessly Lesley scrubbed at something sticky on the small woebe-gone face. It was amazing how Richard Percival, aged barely two, acted like a magnet for anything muddy or gluey or generally messy. With Richie you needed an inordinate love of children or a large plastic pinny, or preferably both.

'Perhaps we should take him with us,'

Lesley wavered. 'You'll have no trouble with Phil, but with this one — '

'I'll cope with him. We'll get along fine! You're supposed to be having a break and a rest, aren't you?'

'Well — ' she wavered still more. 'Anyway, I won't rest after what you've told me! I've been thinking . . . don't be offended, but does Gill know you've inherited this house and some money?'

I looked at her, this time startled beyond argument. Richie wriggled to the floor, bumped his head and started up his usual deafening roar, obliterating something else she said. Possibly it was an apology. I hoped it was.

While Richie was still being hushed, Martin came in. He viewed the pandemonium with accustomed resignation, and bent to kiss Lesley. Tall and bespectacled, he exuded a sort of dreamy tolerance of the world at large.

'Nearly ready, dear?' he asked her mildly, and then turned to me. 'Oh, I saw Gill near the station, he said — now let me get this right — add this list to the car calls for E district — and remind Fred Marshall to be at the station at six . . . and he skipped lunch so he'll be here in ten minutes if you can get something ready? . . . '

I ignored Lesley's very loud and expressive snort in the background. But because the secret was a secret no more, I blurted out, 'You might as well know, Martin! — I'm going to marry him, even though Lesley thinks he's just after my money!'

Not waiting for any answer I stalked out of the room and down the stairs. It wasn't the first time I had crossed swords with my sister. Usually, the cause was far less serious.

The room that had been Dad's bedroom had become a convenient office: a table was stacked with papers, posters, canvassing records, lists clipped on boards. The computer and printer had a desk to themselves. It was in this room last night that Myron had asked the still unbelievable question: 'Will you do me the honour of marrying me? . . . ' It was like him to phrase it that way. More than anyone I had ever known he could always find words, effortlessly, gracefully. And that was no crime! — though Lesley seemed to think it was . . .

I dealt with the addresses, and then rang Fred Marshall, who always needed a little prodding. He assured me, 'Right, Miss Barrington, tell Gill I'll be there on the dot!'

Everyone used that familiar abbreviation. It came as naturally as addressing me with strict formality. But from the start, to him I had been 'Thelma', to me he had been 'Myron'.

In the kitchen I began preparing soup and sandwiches. A large, rather bare kitchen it was, with red-tiled floor and some of its walls peeling a little. This whole place needed a makeover. Well, it could be done! I had the resources — and now the incentive as well . . .

'Thelma, excuse me — ' Martin's quiet voice spoke from the doorway. (He always sounded apologetic: Lesley

was for ever chiding his self-effacement.)
'I wanted to give you this, to thank you for having the boys. Lesley does so need a real break . . . '

He was offering a small package, which disclosed a boxed set of Elgar recordings. I protested, 'I don't want a present for looking after the children!'

'I know. But — I think you'll like this . . . so please will you take it?'

'Of course,' I said more gently. 'I'm sure I'll like it.'

'If Richie lets you enjoy it.' He smiled, but the smile merged into new anxiety as he laid the little package on the kitchen table where a few election leaflets were scattered — they migrated to every corner of the house, I was sure they were privately breeding — with Myron's photograph looking up at us. 'Les was just telling me . . . I believe she said a bit too much to you, she's in rather a stressed state . . . '

'Oh, don't apologise, I knew what she'd think! What do *you* think?'

'Me? Oh, I — I — ' He looked mildly

scandalised. 'I wouldn't presume to interfere.'

'But I'm asking your opinion. You did know Myron before I did!'

'Not for long. Of course, Lesley's still sore because of the Hanley's job, but I didn't even fancy it — far more Gill's cup of tea than mine, he's much more of a go-getter — '

As Martin was backing to the door, clearly anxious to escape, we heard someone arriving in the outside porch. He said at once, 'Who's that? — I'll go!'

I realised he hadn't answered my difficult question at all.

Voices came to me from the hallway, one soft and rapid and unmistakable. 'Good, you're still here! — when do you leave?'

'Oh, when we're ready. It's only a few steps round to the station — '

'No taxi booked? — that won't do! Tell Lesley I'll drive you.'

'It really isn't necessary — ' Martin began, and then gave in. 'Thanks, Gill.'

His footsteps retreated upstairs. That

other voice called, 'Thelma?'

'In the kitchen,' I called back. Stupidly my hands were shaking. This wasn't the first time I had seen him on this busy day, but he had been in and out, touring round the Constituency, always with other people.

'Hello!' he said simply.

He was a man you might pass in a crowd unnoticed: about my own height (if I wore my inevitable flat heels), his features regular enough. The one outstanding attribute was his thick, straight hair of a shade the female weeklies would call 'brightest copper' or 'fiery sunset' — with eyes, in contrast, very dark. The photo on the table portrayed all that. It couldn't add the vitality and energy, the brilliant, restless personality, the laughter in those changeful eyes that could glow with fierce enthusiasm or melt into gentle, intimate appeal.

The last was perhaps the real secret. That, along with the gift of impassioned oratory which could change in an instant to quiet simplicity, making each member of an audience feel he spoke to them alone. But now there was no audience. Just the two of us.

I answered, 'Hello! This is just ready. Are you in a rush?'

'Always in a rush.' He laughed in gentle mockery of my nervousness. 'Don't look so alarmed. I've brought you a little present. A special little present!'

'Another present? Martin just gave me something for helping them out . . .'

'That was kind. But see if you like mine better.'

Inside the small package he offered I found a box. A jeweller's box. Within, nestling on velvet, a diamond and two opals reflected the light. Gazing at the most attractive ring I was astonished — perhaps dismayed, perhaps even more almost angered. I stood in silence.

'What's wrong?' he asked. 'Surely you're not superstitious about opals?'

'No, I'm not. It's a beautiful ring . . .'

'Well, then. You know I don't let grass

grow under my feet.'

There was a difference between letting whole acres of meadowland sprout and taking for granted so huge a decision. I said seriously, 'I said I'd think it over. That's all I said.'

'I know you did. I've saved you the time and trouble.' He was very close to me, his dark eyes looking into mine as he sought my bare left hand. 'Let's see if it fits. I can get it altered if necessary . . . '

I clenched the hand, resisting him. Thomas Barrington's eldest daughter, with much of her father's solid strength of character, not to say obstinacy, couldn't be cajoled or bullied so easily. Always I resented my life being handed to me in a package. Only with those eyes hurt and appealing on mine, it was hard not to surrender.

'You could have waited for a 'yes', we need to talk about a few things. Do you know my age, for a start?'

'Does it matter?' His fingers were softly, insistently, unclenching mine.

'And I'm no good at dressing up, meeting people, and making polite conversation — '

'I asked you to be my wife, not my hostess with the mostest. You've been speaking to Lesley, haven't you?' His quick, shrewd judgment startled me, though I had met it many times before. 'Thelma, it's your life, not hers.'

'That's what I told her — ' I started involuntarily, and then stopped short, angered still more at betraying the argument. I tried to pull away from him, but he was holding me fast.

Very gently he remonstrated, 'Why make it so difficult? Isn't it the simplest thing in the world? I love you, I want to be with you for the rest of our lives . . . and you do care for me a little, don't you? . . . '

How could I deny it? He must know, when he knew so much.

'Then where's the problem? A few extra years don't matter, I know how you've used them — and now the sun can come out for you. Don't hide from it, don't stay under the grey clouds . . . '

The vivid words he could employ so readily were more meaningful because of shafts of sunlight streaming into the kitchen, turning to a blaze of fire his copper-hued hair, striking sparks from the ring that had slipped easily on to my finger.

'This will be a wonderful summer,' he said. 'A golden summer. Believe me.'

I did believe. His arms enclosed me, his lips found mine, and there were no more words. I clung to him, carried suddenly beyond those shadowed years of longing sternly repressed, of emptiness seeming beyond redemption.

I closed my eyes because I didn't need to see the radiance slanting through the window. That was for all the world to share. This sunburst, this new golden dawn, was mine alone.

* * *

Richie's plaintive wail on the stairs warned me the Percivals were coming down. I was trying to look composed and businesslike when Lesley appeared. But she wasn't deceived — and I declined descending to the indignity of hiding my left hand with its unaccustomed adornment. She commented, 'Well! Things have been happening here.'

Myron said quietly, 'Show her, Thelma.'

She took my extended hand, clearly fighting her impulse to speak out too plainly. Something like incredulous dismay was written on her face.

'Very nice. I hope you'll be happy. I *hope* you will . . . '

I bent my head for her sombre little peck on my cheek. Martin kissed me too, mumbling something unintelligible, and held out a hand to Myron with obvious sincerity.

'All the very best to you. To you both.'

'There's one way you could help us,' Myron suggested. 'We'll be one big happy family — so can you persuade your wife I'm not the scallywag she thinks I am?'

Martin gave an embarrassed little laugh. Lesley, meeting Myron's eyes full and square, almost relaxed into an answering smile and hastily twitched it from her face. She said sharply, 'Let's get ready, Martin. I don't relish this journey, without missing the train!'

'Wouldn't a plane have been easier?' Myron queried.

'Just now I don't fancy airports and planes, nor long car journeys. We've done the night sleeper before, and it's fine. And we're stopping off first to spend an hour with that relation of Dad's — it's her ninety-eighth birthday, she probably won't even recognise us . . . '

'Okay. That's kind of you. So can't I drive you to her place, or to Euston?'

'You're much too busy. We've just one wheeled suitcase — and I may resemble the back of a bus but I can still move. Thanks all the same!'

Behind her back Myron looked at me

with a part-comic, part-rueful grimace.

There was an interval while he disposed of his meal, and Lesley gave me more instructions about Richie, and then Myron dashed out again briefly. He returned just as Leslie was donning her coat to tell her, 'Your carriage awaits, Madame, no arguments!'

In the porch, a mild breeze came in to us, an assorted group of people involved in their own cross currents. Amid the chorus of goodbyes I detached Richie from Martin. His hot little hands gripped, his face was wet against my neck. Beyond the gate Myron's car stood at the kerb, a sky-blue convertible which you could possibly call 'flashy'? . . . While Martin loaded the luggage I watched Myron help my sister very carefully into her seat.

With a face of supreme innocence he asked her, 'You did remember to vote today?'

'I meant to! I've been rushed off my feet.'

'Then we'll stop on the way, it won't take a moment . . . and that's *not* why I offered the lift!'

Lesley's manner had scarcely melted. To me alone she unbent, to call in farewell, 'Give Phil our love, we'll send lots of postcards . . . and take care of yourself, Thelma.'

'I will,' I promised. 'Don't worry about the boys. Just have a good rest.'

The car moved off rapidly. I was left standing there, the sun on my face, Richie in my arms. There was a last glimpse of Lesley and Martin both waving, and then the curve of The Crescent hid them. In the quiet there were only Richie's sobs.

In readiness for this I had bought him a present, and he was cheered up by a bus driver's set, including badge and plastic steering wheel with attached hooter. While he ran a fleet of buses up and down the hall with hooter obligato, I found the kitchen — without Myron's transforming presence — again a rather dreary room reeking of soup.

But Myron, and Myron's magic, would be back.

It was perhaps as well the following time was too busy for realisation of all that had happened today. We weren't alone for long, with people in and out, phone calls, a running buffet of tea and biscuits. Presently I slipped round to the school to collect Phil, a serious nearly-six and quite amazingly resembling his father. I bought the boys ices on the way back, and made sure to give them a special tea and as much attention as I could. But efforts to get them to bed at their usual times didn't work out, with all the toing and froing: they ended up watching a favourite film which Lesley had left handy for emergencies. It distracted them from thoughts of their parents.

Eventually, when they were more or less settled down in their room — Richie clutching as always a threadbare soft toy of doubtful species — people were gathering downstairs over coffee and snacks to chat and compare notes, two or three going on presently to witness the vote counting. Of course, the children's presence made that impossible for me. But already I found news of my engagement to Myron was getting known, and there were profuse — if surprised — con-gratulations.

Fred Marshall, bald and perspiring and devastatingly cheery, had discov-ered it earlier and now produced some bottles of wine, like a conjurer exhibit-ing a rabbit.

'Here we go, ladies and gents! We'll drink to the happy couple, eh? Got any glasses, Miss Barrington? — '

I found some, and they were soon circulating. There were just two refus-als. One was our local Treasurer, Miss Baynes, a vinegary lady who looked as though she suspected the drinks had come out of the funds. The other was Myron, who had just arrived. That didn't surprise me, remembering other times when an evening's leafleting had ended in a bar.

'Come on, Gill,' Fred Marshall remonstrated, 'this is an occasion! . . . Here's to a big vote after all our hard work, eh? — '

The words were echoed and glasses raised. The cheery Fred tried to push one into Myron's hand, and it was rejected so sharply that the glass fell and splashed the carpet and my feet. Myron walked away, leaving Fred to welter in apologies while I fetched a cloth to clean up.

The assemblage was breaking up, cars starting along The Crescent. Mr. Weaver, our local Chairman and a prosperous silver-haired City type, thanked me for my hospitality and help. Miss Baynes asked me to submit a chit for expenses, her glance adding a warning to scale the sum well down.

'What will you do now?' Myron asked me in the hall.

'Clear up this chaos. Then go to bed.'

'My prosaic Thelma. Shall I call in later with the result?'

'I'll be asleep long before then,' I

said, though I doubted it.

'Sorry about that fool Marshall. Why can't he mind his own business? Am I accountable to cheerful idiots like him for everything I do —? '

I whispered a restraining 'Ssh!' — aware of Miss Baynes at my elbow. I watched them leave together. It was a beautiful night, street lamps glimmering between those fairytale cherry trees. I called to him, 'Goodnight, good luck!' and saw his parting smile.

Indoors, the house was silent and strange. After restoring some sort of order, I went upstairs to peep at the sleeping boys. Phil's hair was dark against a pale pillow, his school bag placed neatly aside. Richie was an angel in repose.

In my bedroom I undressed wearily. I laid the opal ring back in its box. When the light was turned off, it seemed I could still see it glimmering in the darkness.

2

Overnight a note reached my letterbox headed *'An unearthly hour and home-ward bound, didn't want to wake you.'* Underneath Myron had scribbled the voting figures — with his name prominently in third place, not too far behind the leaders. For a first attempt campaign largely self-organised, a personal triumph.

On the early news a political commentator summarised: *'Note the achievement by an energetic young man, Myron Gillespie — a new name, one we shall certainly hear again . . . '*

A thrill of pride rose within me. It would be my place to provide an anchor for that volatile nature perhaps lacking perseverance. Sipping my early tea, I read once more the second part of the scribbled note:

'I'll collect you around nine . . . we'll drive down to Brighton so you can meet my family . . . '

It was easy to speak airily of collecting me. There were, of course, the boys.

However, Mrs. White opposite, whose son Jack was Phil's friend and who interchanged with Lesley on 'school runs', hopefully would fetch Phil this afternoon and keep him till I returned. Maybe she would take Richie too on this rather special occasion.

Having watched her husband leave for the station, I slipped across to ask. Kay White, about Lesley's age with a youthful ponytail of dark hair, greeted me with surprise. In her very modern kitchen Jack was spooning up cornflakes. She commented brightly about the voting: 'I knew he'd do well, Miss Barrington, he's got what it takes! . . . '

Plainly she was amazed — not to say knock-flat astounded — to hear of our engagement, though she tried to cover it up. Phil was no problem, she said, and she would have taken Richie too except for a dentist appointment and a promised call on a sick friend.

I said I could manage. In any case, it was unpardonable to dump the children the day after their parents' departure — so if I went out today, Richie must come too.

The boys were just stirring after their late night, and there followed a pantomime of getting up and getting breakfast. Richie wept for his absent Mummy, and upset his Kryspy-Pops in floods of milk, which meant a change of clothes. A wistful Phil was ready for school on time, and I waved goodbye as Kay White set off with him, her lively Jack chattering away. Probably the company would help Phil along.

Again this was a beautiful day, warm as summer, and there faced me the problem of what to wear for this fairly alarming first meeting. A slender navy-and-white dress, nicely fitting and virtually unworn, might fit the bill, together with new white sandals.

Low-heeled sandals. I took thrice the usual time over my hair.

While I was dressing Richie found a container of rainwater by the kitchen door. It meant his third set of clothes in under two hours.

Myron's somewhat flamboyant car was just gliding into the kerb, today with its convertible top open and its driver sporting a leaf-green tee-shirt and designer sunglasses. Both vehicle and occupant might have escaped from a glossy holiday brochure. I looked out at them with a sense of complete unreality.

But my greeting was matter of fact. First, congratulations on last night. Second, today's trip must needs be a threesome.

'Thelma, surely there must be *some-one*? . . . I don't want to be unreasonable, but — '

'Sorry. We could postpone it till his Mum gets back. Or you could go on your own, of course.'

'Thanks, I didn't plan to go on my own. All right, load him up!'

Ready to hand was the car-seat I sometimes needed in my own vehicle. As it happened, my car had been damaged recently while it was parked, causing all sorts of problems. It wasn't yet back on the road.

Fitting the seat in place, Myron smiled at Richie kindly enough, and even promised to buy him a bucket and spade — which proved Lesley's opinions were all unfounded. Almost she had made me doubt my own judgment. I wouldn't doubt it again. A sudden tide of joy came to me, a casting-off of care.

As we set out, Kay White was just leaving too. We ended by giving her a lift to the nearby dentist, and she sat next to Myron, chattering brightly.

'This is some car, Harry would give his eye-teeth for it! . . . Sorry about Richie, tomorrow or Sunday I'd have taken him . . . '

'It's difficult visiting my folks on summer weekends. They own a café, you see.'

'Really? We often run down there, we might know it? — '

'A bit off the beaten track. A board outside says 'Try Grandma Pearson's Home Cooking'.'

'Oh, I'm sure we've seen it, I'll ask Harry. What a small world! . . . '

At the dentist's she left us regretfully. Myron's gaze followed her bobbing ponytail and her shapely figure.

He asked me to move into the front beside him, but I needed to stay with Richie. Myron gave a little grunt, and we swept on our way. As always he drove fast, with a careless skill. Three times his mobile phone trilled, and after that he switched it off: 'On vacation!' he commented.

I exclaimed suddenly, 'Oh, I left mine behind, it was such a rush leaving — '

'Doesn't matter. Now no-one can disturb us. The day is ours!'

It did matter, if Lesley or Jan wanted to contact me.

I was looking at people in other cars, especially one we passed twice and each time caught us up again. The girl had classic features and flowing blonde hair. I was blonde too, as far as that went — but she appeared so elegant and serene. The wind was loosening untidy strands of my hair, and Richie's moist hands clung to me as his first excitement gave way to boredom. Richie's boredoms were vocal affairs. One wailing complaint became urgent.

We turned into a convenient garage with a cloakroom. But worse was to come.

'Feel sick,' he announced ominously. 'Auntie Felma, feel *sick* . . . '

'You'll be fine, Richie. Just don't think about it.'

But his face was assuming a grey and ghastly look. Too late I remembered Lesley's unhappy experiences with car travel.

'Myron, quick! — we'll have to stop! — '

'Hang on.' He accelerated sharply. 'There's a lay-by just along here . . . '

The few moments required to reach

it were a few too many.

Myron swore briefly and not mildly, which he didn't often do. I tried to comfort Richie, and attempted vainly to mop up with tissues as we stopped in the lay-by.

'I'm sorry. Richie really couldn't help it . . . '

Myron did seem more concerned about his car than about Richie — or the luckless dress I so carefully selected this morning. I repeated, 'I'm sorry! . . . Have you got anything I could use to clean up a bit?'

He handed me a couple of this morning's newspapers, and then left the car and leant on a gate, leaving me to it. I did the best I could. It wasn't the moment to mention that the papers possibly carried a by-election story.

When we set off again I said hopefully, 'He looks better, I think he's over it now.'

'Shouldn't think he's got anything left,' Myron observed.

Nevertheless, I was on tenterhooks

until we reached the outskirts of the sprawling seaside town. It was then, seeing houses and shops and people, that I suddenly realised what a sad state I was in to visit anybody, let alone a first meeting with future in-laws. I muttered, 'I don't know what they'll think. I can't walk in like this.'

He glanced round at me, regaining his good humour. 'Then buy something new.'

'Shall I? Perhaps it would be a good idea.'

He stopped outside a big fashion shop (invariably sailing straight into a parking space just vacated) and pointed to a model in one of the windows. 'That one!'

'The pink one? I never wear pink.'

'Be a devil, live a little! Here you are.' He pressed some notes into my hand. 'Only that one, mind. And — please, take Richie with you?'

After visiting the washroom to clean Richie up (luckily I had brought along yet another outfit for him) I hoped the shop wouldn't have my size in the pink model. But they did, and I tried it on — and had to admit, surveying a mirror, that perhaps that soft muted cerise did something for me. The skirt was long and swirly. I chose too a white cardigan, and a flimsy, floaty white scarf with just a hint of matching colour. Transformed, I stepped out again into the sunshine.

As I fastened Richie back in his seat, Myron regarded me gravely and then leant across to pull out two or three hair grips.

'Oh, what are you doing? It takes ages to fasten that up nicely — '

'Then don't. Tie it in a bunch with that scarf. You have very pretty hair.'

'Have I?' I whispered.

We turned a corner or two and came within sight of the sea, blue and sparkling under a serene cloudless sky. Ahead of us were several side turnings, and somewhere among them I saw a café frontage, a little shabby but bright with potted geraniums and red-check curtains. A painted sign extolled the home cooking of Grandma Pearson.

Richie had started clamouring for the promised bucket and spade. Myron said, 'I don't know about the spade. The bucket might be handy on the way home? . . . '

★ ★ ★

Lesley was right in saying that though I had spent so much time recently with Myron, really I knew little of his personal history: only that his father had died some years ago, and he had grown up here in this rather unlikely setting with his mother and her parents. In picturing Mrs. Gillespie I had imagined someone quite young and attractive with his charming smile and fire-bright hair. It was a surprise, as he edged the car into the café's rear yard, when two ladies hurried out to greet him. You had to doubt, just for an instant, which was which.

But of course, the plump one was 'Grandma Pearson', her round, kindly, blue-eyed face hot and shiny, her bare feet in worn slippers. Myron's mother, in contrast, was beanpole thin, dried-up and washed-out, with nervous twisting hands. Her dark hair was heavily silvered. Only her eyes were like his, bright and dark.

Both the ladies embraced him rapturously. A mild little elderly man in the background, very wiry and active, beamed and wiped his hands on a long blue apron. It occurred to me that Grandma Pearson could almost pick her husband up and tuck him under one arm.

They were all pouring out words of welcome: 'Myron, *lovely* to see you! . . . we so *hoped* you'd come! . . . you *can* stay all day, can't you?'

Myron laughed and agreed, 'Absolutely all day. But I didn't come alone.' He held out a hand to me. 'Stand up and be recognised, Thelma darling.'

'Oh, so you're Thelma!' Grandma enclosed me at once in effusive arms that almost squeezed away my breath.

'We've heard all about you, love! — Myron can't always get down to see us, but he phones and sends notes and cards . . . so we knew you were getting engaged, we've been *longing* to meet you! . . . Look, Evie, what a lovely ring! . . . Look, Fred! . . . ?'

As my left hand was held up for public scrutiny, Richie suddenly decided he had been awed to silence long enough. Myron explained his presence in a few words, and added, 'He was a bit ill in the car coming along. Grandma, you wouldn't do us a little favour — ?'

'Oh no!' I interrupted, quite aghast. 'I'll do it, Mrs. Pearson!'

'You don't want to spoil that pretty dress, you leave it to me. Go inside with Myron, just make yourself at home! . . . Richie, you come with Grandma and see what she's got for you. Poor little chap to have such a naughty tummy . . . '

I was borne into the house, suddenly part of this family of strangers. In a warm, cluttered room, with bright curtains and covers and several plants in coloured pots, I was settled in a big armchair. Between visits to the adjoining café where evidently their helper 'Cheryl' ('unreliable, but good when she wants to be' Grandma whispered) was holding the fort, they kept on talking. They repeated how exciting it was to hear and see Myron's name in the media. They asked how his wonderful job in London was going. More awkward were questions about the two of us, when would the wedding be, where would we live.

'No problems,' Myron said, 'we've a big house to live in. But I daresay we'll sell it, it should fetch a tidy sum. We need only a small flat, just the two of us . . .'

It was the first intimation I had of the future destiny of my property.

Yet in a way I was coming to understand Myron's way of doing just what he wanted with everyone and everything. Obviously these people had indulged his every whim over the years. Perhaps I was making excuses for him to cover a stirring uneasiness: certainly I would have something pointed to say to him later about announcing our engagement to the family before even asking me to marry him — and almost selling my house over my head . . .

There was just one thing to be very thankful for. The Pearson/Gillespies might well have been wildly jealous of me. But it seemed if Myron wanted me then I must be made much of, for his sake.

The requirements of the café trade — evidenced by Cheryl, a crossgrained-looking woman in a state of rising indignation poking her head round the door — cut short that first difficult meeting. We must have lunch there in the back room, Grandma said as she bustled away: just the two of us — and of course Richie, who was exploring a box of old toys she had produced. It was little Mr. Pearson who brought us a tray of the 'home cooking', smiling on us widely and constantly.

I was in no mood to enjoy the meal,

and Richie rebelled after a few mouthfuls and went back to the toys. I sat awkwardly opposite Myron.

He asked, 'What do you think of them?'

'I like them a lot. They must work very hard here, don't they?'

'They work their socks off. I don't mind hard work — you should know that by now — but drudgery like this would drive me round the twist. I can't stand being tied down. Of course, it'll be different when I have you to come home to.'

I was looking with interest around that pleasant, homely room, and a photograph on the mantelpiece caught my eye: a wedding group, strangely pushed half behind a vase as though in concealment. The bride was a much younger Evelyn Gillespie. The man beside her could easily have been mistaken for Myron.

I exclaimed, 'You're a carbon copy of him!'

'I hope not. The less said about him the better.'

'That's — your father?'

'My father. All right, I'll tell you the story. He walked out on Mum soon after I was born, she moved in here and she's been here ever since. He found another poor trusting woman — or women . . . but periodically he turned up here. When he was sober he could charm an angel out of heaven. He'd spin Mum a pitiful tale and she gave him all the money she had. When he was drinking he had the vilest temper — well, let's skip the details.'

'Then *that*'s why you never touch . . . ' I whispered in sudden enlightenment. 'And now he's dead?'

'Yes, and Mum won't have a word said against him. The last time I saw him I was just a kid, I was fixing my bike out in the yard after school when he walked in. The others were all busy in the café. It was one of his bad days, I called him a — well, never mind what I called him. He grabbed up one of the bike tools and said he'd stop my insolence. When I started bleeding like

48

a stuck pig he got frightened and made off . . . and no one knows to this day, no one except you. Our secret, yes?'

'Of course.' I was utterly shocked. 'But — when they found you were hurt? — '

'Ah. I knew what it would do to Mum, for some reason she still cared about him . . . so I rode my bike bang-smack at the gatepost. There were some crates of empty bottles piled up, the whole lot caved in — I was pulled out half-dead. No one suspected anything. I said the brakes failed.'

'That was quite a wonderful thing to do.'

'You think so? I still hadn't recovered when we heard he'd collapsed in the street — maybe he was ill when it all happened, I suppose you could give him the benefit of the doubt. Mum visited him in the hospital, she swears he knew her before the end. That meant a lot to her. And that's my pretty family story.'

There was such a great contrast

between his life and mine! I had known sickness and loss, but never fear, violence, disillusion. Now my future was to be joined with his, I longed to comfort him for a darkened past I had never dreamed of in the brightness of his today.

I was still seeking words when there was a sound at the door, and Myron shook his head at me in quick warning to stay silent. Mr. Pearson brought in a tray of coffee, beaming on us benevolently. But just as he left, he turned to offer Myron an envelope.

'Oh, I was forgetting — that's for you, boy. Came this morning. We meant to post it on if you couldn't come down.'

My mind still full of all I had just heard, I paid little heed to that minor matter. Vaguely, I thought Myron's face betrayed disquiet. He said abruptly, 'Excuse me a moment!' and left the room. It was just a little odd.

Soon after came a brief but awkward tête-à-tête with Evie Gillespie, who sat down with me to talk non-stop about Myron: ever a wonderful son, always loving and considerate to his family. She hoped I would help in all his enterprises, provide unlimited background support. Plainly she saw my role as one of selfless devotion.

The episode was cut short when Myron suggested we go out a while until the lunch period was through. There was no rush to return to London. I agreed uncertainly, remembering Phil.

At a nearby shop Richie was delighted by a plastic bucket and spade, and we were soon crunching along the shingle of a sunny beach to find a resting place. At a distance the Pier basked under the bright sky. Inquisitive gulls strutted and foraged. With Richie busy filling bucketfuls of pebbles, I tried to will all anxieties from my mind — to feel only the sun and the sea breeze, the joy of the child, the peace of this moment.

I asked Myron to tell me about last

night, but he answered lazily, 'Another time, today is just for us.' He had, of course, slept very little. He was lying full length beside me, in rare peace and silence. But instantly he was aware of a possible catastrophe when a child floating on a blow-up frog drifted to deeper water and toppled off. His lightning reaction was to run down the beach with the clear intention of rescue — which alerted other people to the danger, and a couple of bathers got there first. The child was frightened but more or less unharmed. Her young mother, disturbed from texting on her phone, was near hysterics — and it was Myron who calmed her down, placated an outraged old gentleman in a deckchair, and generally restored order.

'Whew!' He returned to me when it was over. 'I thought I'd get a bit wet.'

I said sincerely, 'I'm impressed!'

'That's nice.' He settled down again and stretched luxuriously. 'You know, I might run a campaign on water safety — swimming pools, rivers, beaches

. . . the time's coming when you hear of too many accidents. We can highlight the cause of every child who wakes on a sunny morning — and might never see that sun set . . . '

Despite the gravity of the subject I hinted, 'I thought today was 'just for us'?'

'Sorry. But it's important.'

'I know. So will you wait while I find my notebook and pen, Mr. Gillespie — to add it to your More Beauty in Local Parks campaign, and Cleaner Food Means Emptier Hospitals, and Shopping Buddies for the Elderly — etc. etc.?'

'Isn't it all worthwhile? It just needs handling with imagination. Believe me.'

'I do believe you. I'm with you!'

'Then why are you winding me up?' He rolled over to look at me reproachfully.

'Because I like listening to you. I really do!'

Perhaps it was the effect of that disturbing personal story he confided earlier, the shadows lurking behind his sometimes over-the-top self confidence, that was drawing me closer to him. And I would soon learn to understand him more and more. As though reading my thoughts he asked out of the blue, 'How soon can we get married?'

'How *soon*? There's no great hurry, is there?'

'Nor any need to wait. I'll tell my landlady what she can do with her top floor back any time you like — the grasping old witch.'

'Oh! Well, I'm not even used to being engaged yet,' I protested half seriously.

His hands captured both mine, the soft persuasive voice was very near to me. 'We don't want a big fuss, do we? Just quick and quiet?'

'All right. Say — six months?' I pulled the answer out of the air.

'Thelma, dearest Thelma. Wouldn't weeks be better? — next month, if we can fix it?'

'Well — ' I still wavered. A wedding in the vague future was different from a pinned-down, imminent wedding. But he stopped all objections by gently pulling my face towards his. His lips sought mime, warm and strong and searching.

It was an interlude timeless and unbelievable. Always the sunshine on a sparkling sea, the cries of children at play, would bring it back to me. I knew Lesley was doubly wrong, wrong about him, wrong about me.

For how could this overwhelming tide of new feelings be anything but true love?

* * *

We bought Richie some ice-cream, and I chose a few gifts to take home: a pretty shell box for Lesley, a novelty pen for Martin, some crayons for Phil. For once I was like those other carefree couples strolling happily hand in hand. That was unbelievable too.

We found a vacant bench while Richie finished off the ice-cream that wasn't smeared around the landscape. Keeping well out of range, Myron said dubiously, 'I daren't think of the ride back. I'm afraid I haven't much patience with kids, except in small doses.'

Even a momentary stab of dismay — recalling long-standing dreams of a family of my own to cherish and work for, bringing a fulfilment my life had lacked — didn't last long. Later, much later, if he hadn't changed his mind, surely I could change it for him? Maybe poor Richie hardly seemed an urgent invitation to parenthood . . .

'There's something I wanted to ask you,' Myron was saying with unusual hesitation. 'Only — I don't know if I dare.'

'Come on, that's nonsense. You've nerve enough for anything!'

'Not for this. I don't want to spoil today . . . ' His eyes were suddenly avoiding mine. 'Could you lend me some money?'

I said, utterly taken aback. 'I could. How much?'

'Say — a couple of thousand? Or — a bit more? — '

'*How* much?'

'Sorry. I did warn you. Look, let's forget about it!'

'No. If you need it, I'll sort out a cheque tonight. Is something wrong? — I think I'm entitled to know.'

'It's just — I owe someone. You're very sweet and very generous, and I promise you'll get it back.'

'I don't want it back. I'd just like to know,' I insisted, very much my late father's daughter, 'how you can hand out an expensive ring one day — and a pricey fashion-store dress the next — and urgently need two thousand pounds.' And then, as he was still silent, with a rare frown making his face all at once older, I had a flash of inspiration, almost intuition. 'Or didn't you know until just now? — was it that letter your Grandad gave you?'

He was angry and he was disturbed. But the smile triumphed, as mostly it did.

'You're remarkably bright. Top marks! It's just an unpaid account that's caught up with me. Very reprehensible I know, so don't lecture me, ma'am.'

He wasn't going to explain. Unless I might perhaps drag the details out of him — and so ruin this dreamlike day. It was quite feasible that he had run into debt: he had extravagant ideas — as Miss Baynes could testify, guarding the working fund as though with her life. But he was holding down the well remunerated job at Hanley's which had caused so much trouble. Perhaps his mind was so full of splendid ideals that something so mundane as settling accounts just slipped his notice.

Well, I would set things straight this time. After all, nothing was really changed: the sun still shone, the sea still sparkled. Gladly I turned back to mopping up the last of Richie's ice-cream.

'I imagine his Mum is enjoying some blessed peace,' Myron said. 'No wonder she gets a bit niggly. Shall we make a move?'

As we were collecting our bits and pieces, a family settled down nearby, turning on a rather raucous radio. I retrieved Richie's bucket, and then was suddenly still. News headlines, snatches of a grave voice announcing them, burst upon me.

' . . . *it is now believed that three people lost their lives and at least twenty were injured in the rail accident near Glasgow earlier today . . . a spokesman said the line will remain closed until . . . '*

My breath caught in a little gasp. Myron said softly, 'Scotland is a big place. Lots of railways, lots of people.'

'I know. But — they're part of some poor families . . . '

'Come on.' He got quickly to his feet. 'We've been out much longer than I meant — and Mum will be waiting for us. Ups-a-daisy, Richie!'

Richie had set up his usual wail of 'Carry!' and Myron lifted him uncomplainingly. I trailed along with the buggy filled with a jumble of bags, glad to be moving because I was suddenly chilled through in my flimsy new dress.

'There's Grandad,' Myron said suddenly. 'That's odd! — '

Fred Pearson looked different without his businesslike apron, a forlorn little figure peering up and down, clearly looking for someone or something. Myron muttered something about being an idiot to leave his mobile turned off so long, that possibly all the excitement had triggered one of his mother's 'turns'.

'I'll run on ahead and see what's wrong. Can you bring the kid?'

He set the protesting child down and dived across the road, weaving unnervingly through the traffic. On the opposite pavement Mr. Pearson hailed him with huge relief.

I strapped Richie into the buggy. Myron's fears were totally different from mine . . . but the chill now possessing me was like a shroud of ice.

3

It always seemed to me afterwards, looking back on that brightest of days which changed so suddenly to waking nightmare, that I knew what had happened long before I was told. Certainly I learnt little from Grandad Pearson in the breathless minutes it took us to reach the café. There had been an urgent phone call for me, he said. Someone called Mrs. White — and no, it was nothing to do with Phil. There was some news from Scotland.

At the café two or three people were just leaving their tables and Grandma was sticking a SORRY, WE'RE CLOSED notice on the door. The smell of food brought me sudden nausea.

In the homely back room with its bright curtains, Myron's mother urged me to sit down. As she handed me a telephone, Mrs. Pearson led Richie away.

'I'm so sorry, Thelma. So sorry, dear,' Evelyn Gillespie quavered.

'Please, I just want to *know*!'

'An accident, dear. On the railway . . . '

'We heard about it.' I was calmer than she was. 'Just tell me. My sister? . . . '

'Yes, she was taken to the hospital. But — her husband . . . '

I nodded quickly. Martin, to me the kindest of brothers, would come home no more. I asked as though from miles away, 'How bad is Lesley?'

'The lady didn't say, she was so upset. Let's hope it'll be good news, dear. We — we wrote down the phone numbers . . . '

I was amazed to see how my hand was shaking. Myron took the phone from me without a word.

'Lesley is expecting a baby. Next month,' I told his mother.

'The good Lord save us,' Mrs. Gillespie whispered. 'Another baby?'

'They had names all ready. David

Mark for a boy. Lucie Marina for a girl . . . '

Grandma was bringing in a tray of tea, the chink of the crockery unnaturally loud in the quiet room. Her kind, plump face turned to me full of sympathy. Before she could speak, Myron hushed her quickly.

'Mrs. White? . . . It's Myron, Thelma is here with me . . . Yes, we've been told.'

He gave me the phone. I was aware of his arm around me, warm and gentle. I sat stiffly upright in frozen composure.

Kay White was barely coherent. She found a policeman trying to locate me, she said, after visiting her friend. Phil was back from school, he and Jack were in her garden. Harry was coming home to help. She had no more details about Lesley.

As I was putting the phone down, Myron grabbed it. 'Kay? — yes, I'll look after her and bring her straight home . . . yes, don't worry, I'll get on to the police and the hospital straight away to explain you've contacted us . . . we'll be back as fast as I can make it!'

In the quiet that followed, people spoke and moved. Mrs. Pearson gave me a steaming cup and some aspirins, and to please her I accepted them. There was just one fixed idea in my mind, to get home — to reach Phil.

Myron left the room to make several calls in private. Richie came trotting in with Grandpa Pearson, who had been playing with him. Evie Gillespie kept silently patting my arm. I was aware of everyone's concern, their efforts to comfort and help all far off, beyond the blurring mist of shock.

When at last I went out to the dazzling sunlight in the yard, one thing alone was real. Someone had put my bag in the car with some parcels showing. For Lesley a box decorated with shells. For Martin a fancy pen.

'Are you sure you can manage?' Grandma was asking as she lifted Richie into his seat. 'Thelma, why not leave the little chap with us a few days, if you're rushing straight off to Scotland? We'd treat him like our own, love. We'd take good care of him.'

'It's very good of you. But I'd better get him home,' I whispered. Their kindness, and those parcels, almost were too much.

Myron promised to ring them later. There were hands waving, more offers of help. Mrs. Gillespie stood a little apart like a white-faced ghost. Mr. Pearson's reedy voice called out last of all to Myron, 'Take it steady, boy.'

Thankfully Richie was so tired out by the day's excitements that he slept most of the way. I cradled him, his rumpled hair soft against my face. Myron scarcely spoke as the car ate up the miles, green sunlit countryside slipping past us.

'Martin was . . . he was a good bloke. He seemed so happy.' He broke the silence suddenly. 'He made other people happy — that's something worthwhile. He'd never do harm to a single soul, and everyone knew it . . . '

In the midst of my turmoil I was aware of the intensity of those words. But the impression was quickly lost. I muttered, 'I'll ring Jan to tell them I'm coming tonight.'

'Shall I go with you?'

'Would you? But you're so busy — '

'Hang all that. You come first.'

I thought for a moment. 'No. Perhaps later — but you can't play fast and loose with your job, you've had so much leave lately. But you could help me sort out the journey.'

The quickest and easiest way would be to fly, he said. He would fix it, of course take me to the airport. Already we were nearing home, covering the distance in far less time than it took before.

It seemed strange that The Crescent looked serene and untroubled in its cruel glory of cherry blossom. I felt I had been away for years. Before the car stopped, Kay White came running across, her eyes very red, and Myron spoke to her quietly and comfortingly. In the house I laid Richie, still barely awake, upstairs in his cot.

While Myron searched out flights on the computer, Kay made more of the inevitable tea. Jack and Phil were still in her garden with Harry, she said: she kept on apologising that in her first reaction of shock she couldn't recall where to find us and too late the name of the café came back to her. I told her it had made no real difference. I was quite calm, just trying to plan what to do.

Jan's phone was switched off, likewise Malcolm's, which probably meant they were at the hospital with Lesley. When I tried the house number it was Malcolm's father who spoke to me. I had met him a few times, but hardly knew him: his soft Scottish voice was very kind, offering as much comfort as there was. Martin could scarcely have known what happened, Lesley had serious head injuries. He didn't know about her unborn baby, but everything possible was being done for them both. He would meet me when I could confirm the arrival time. He said poor Jan was longing for me to come.

With the call ended I went upstairs to change out of the flimsy new dress and hang it far back in my wardrobe. I doubted I would ever wear it again.

As an afterthought, I coiled up neatly the long loose tail of my hair. Pretty hair, Myron had said, far back in another world.

* * *

Somehow the task of breaking the news to Phil had to be faced. There was no sense in putting it off. At any moment he would realise I was home, run in to greet me.

'What will you say?' Kay whispered. 'Look, you know you can leave the boys with us, Harry just said to me . . . '

'It's very kind of you both. I'm really grateful. But — Lesley will want to see them.'

'If you do take them both, Thelma,' Myron broke in, 'I'm coming too, no arguments! You're not doing the journey alone with them.'

I was completely undecided. But there was no time to consider, for Harry White had come across the road with Phil. Jack was running straight in until Harry held him back.

It was a shock to see how much Phil was like Martin. He began to ask with his usual grave politeness, 'Did you have a nice time at the seaside, Aunt Thelma?' — and then stopped short. 'What's happened? What's wrong? Is it Richie — ?'

'Richie is sleeping. But there is something wrong. We need to talk about it, Phil.'

Kay mumbled something and hurried out with her own family. I saw Myron melt swiftly away after them

'Come into my bedroom,' I asked Phil. 'You can help me pack a bag.'

'Pack? Why pack? Where are you going?'

'I'm going to stay with your Aunt Jan.'

'Oh, where Mummy and Dad are . . . '

He sat on the edge of the bed beside me, and I put an arm round him. A breeze stirred the curtain gently.

'I knew there was something wrong! — Mrs. White was — well, she was sort of crying when we had tea — and Jack's Dad came home early . . . ' He trailed off, and waited.

Very quietly I told him there had been an accident to a train, that some of the passengers were hurt and some of them died: that his parents had been involved, and his mother was taken to hospital.

'That's where I'm going, to see her. And your Daddy was hurt too, but sometimes — even hospitals can't help people. They — just couldn't make him well again, Phil.'

Stricken eyes looked into mine, bright and dark. Martin's eyes.

'Do you understand?' I whispered. 'About Daddy? . . . '

The child's shocked agony tore into me. His lips moved but no sound came, his eyes were tearless. I groped for more words.

'We have to be very brave, because poor Mummy will need us. You'll help me, won't you? — and Richie, he's only a baby, he'll need you too . . . '

'Can I go with you? To see Mummy?'

'It's a long way away. Wouldn't you like to stay at Jack's home, till she's well enough to talk to you —?'

'No! No, please — please let me come!'

'Of course you can come, darling,' I whispered.

The tears came then, melting the hard wall of pain. I held him close through the first convulsive sobs. After they quietened I didn't hurry him, just holding him, letting the dazed young mind try to understand its loss. At last came a wriggle, a worried question.

'But — but — if she *doesn't* get well . . . what will Richie and me do? . . . '

'You'll still have me. Phil, we'll look forward to having Mummy back home

— but I'll tell you this, so you'll know. Whatever happens, you and Richie will always have a home here with me. Always, always! That's a promise.'

He clung to me and nodded his head. The tears that still flowed were more gentle.

After a while I got up and sorted out a suitcase to pack a few things. Watching me, Phil showed a spark of interest in the journey. How long would we be on the plane, and he had only ever been on one once, and would it be big or small. I took his hand and went softly along to fetch some of his clothes. Richie was still fast asleep.

While we were there the phone rang below in the empty house. I said quickly, 'Stay here, choose a couple of books to take. I shan't be long.'

Still with an armful of his pyjamas and socks I ran down. It was Malcolm's voice — but it had never sounded like this.

'Malcolm, it's Thelma,' I said. And to help him, 'There's some more news?'

'Yes. I don't know how to say it . . . '

The shake in his voice had told me already. Really I had known all along, while I tried to comfort and encourage Phil. Lesley had never regained consciousness, so she had known nothing of Martin's death.

'And — the baby?'

'The baby is alive. She's a little miracle . . . a wee girl. Lucie Marina.'

Lucie Marina. I repeated the name.

Malcolm said Jan was longing to see me. Warned by some small sound, I saw Phil standing there like a statue — so there would be no need to explain this added tragedy. I ended the call quite abruptly.

'She and Daddy are together,' I said softly. 'Phil, we've got each other . . . and we need to look after poor little Richie . . . '

He nodded silently. From above came the whimpers and wails of Richie, just waking.

'Let's go up to him.' I took one small cold hand fast in mine. 'We won't tell him anything now. We'll do it little by little. He's only a baby.'

Phil agreed gravely, 'Only a baby.'

I looked at his face as we went upstairs. For a young child it was an old, old face.

★   ★   ★

The day seemed very chilly after its noontide glory. I was shivering as I climbed again into Myron's car, with the hastily packed bags stowed away.

In the end, we left Richie with the Whites for a few days. We told him his parents weren't well and that was why I had to leave. It had seemed quite a jolly adventure to him, to go to Kay's home with some favourite toys and clothes. Probably she wouldn't have an easy time with him.

During these busy arrangements, with my sorrow of loss held firmly back, I was concerned only with the two little boys whose lives had been laid in ruins. My own future would be dedicated to loving and caring for them, for their own sakes, for the sister I had lost, for Martin who had been my brother. Later would follow memories of this same morning that had brought my own fairy-tale dream briefly so real and near, teasing me with kisses on a breezy beach, with warm arms that held me. But my future belonged now to the children. Not to me — and not to Myron. That resolution already was set in stone.

As the teeming world of the airport received us, Phil was gazing around wide-eyed. Myron had made all the arrangements, and he went on making them, attending to the luggage, leading me to where I should go.

He said, 'Not long to wait. I wish you'd let me come with you . . . but swear to me solemnly, if you need me, let me know? I'll come straight away.'

I nodded, looking into his anxious face that was oddly the face of a stranger. I was completely numb, beyond feeling.

'You've been wonderful,' he said quietly. 'Really wonderful. — Oh, I spoke to John and gave him the address to contact you — '

'John?'

'John Challoner. Martin's friend at work.' He lowered his voice still more. 'He'll want to be at the funeral. He and Martin were — good mates.'

'I know, I've met him — just vaguely. Look, don't waste time hanging about here. Please go back and check on Richie. And I didn't leave a note for the milkman . . . and make sure my car's okay, and tell Mrs. Bailey at No. 33 I can't get her shopping . . . '

'I'll get her shopping. I'll look after everything. But I do so hate having to say goodbye to you . . . '

His gentle sympathy would break down my composure if I let it. For a long silent moment he held me close in farewell. Pain sternly repressed gave a great heave, and I clung to him . . . because suddenly now came clear understanding that this parting could well be for always. Beyond today's loss would follow a clash of loyalties, a conflict of loves. The children or the man, mother to them or wife to him. Not both, not with Myron? . . .

As I was turning away, his hand on my arm held me back. 'Just before you go — ' he said, and then stopped.

'Yes?'

'Oh, this is awful, saying this to you now! Only — you did promise that cheque? . . . '

In the rush of events I had completely forgotten that. It was a petty thing, after all that had happened. I pulled my chequebook from my bag.

'You can have it now. Are you sure that amount will cover it?'

'I think so. Bless you!'

'You *think* so?' I spoke with a severity born of jangled nerves. 'Please make sure, because I don't want to make a practice of this!'

'Of course not. And I'll pay you back, it's just a loan.' His hand was held out, waiting for the cheque, but for a moment I didn't surrender it.

'My father brought us up to be a bit careful about borrowing. He tried never to owe anything all his life — '

'It's a pity I can't say the same about mine.'

'Oh.' The tirade died on my lips. 'Sorry. I didn't mean to preach at you.'

'I deserve the sermon, don't I? I'll try not to deserve another one.'

His fingers slipped the cheque from mine. He kissed me, and spoke a kind word of farewell to Phil. Then he had merged into the crowd. I felt suddenly very alone.

We were soon on the plane, heading steadily North through tranquil evening clouds. Phil was thrilled just at first to gaze through the window, but thankfully exhaustion drifted him into sleep, closing his dark bewildered eyes still smeared with their tears.

I sat watching him, wondering whether Richie was sleeping too. I thought of Lesley and Martin leaving for their holiday, the car slipping away along The Crescent. It was so cruel that almost to the last moment Lesley and I had exchanged sharp words, because I was so angry about her too outspoken opinion of Myron.

Now she would never know whether she was right or wrong. And maybe I wouldn't know either. His soaring ideals and packed schedules left little room for encumbrances: only today, had he not admitted that he tolerated children only in small doses? Could I really expect him to take on a ready-made dependent family, two young boys and — if heaven were kind — a frail newborn baby girl as well? . . .

No tears or regrets could bring back my sister and her husband. But the sacred promise I gave Phil in the first groping anguish of his bereavement must never be retracted. Never, never retracted!

★　★　★

No welcome could have been more warm and caring than that the Fraser family gave us that night.

Of recent years I had seen far too

little of Janine, being so occupied with Dad's illness, divided from her by distance and responsibilities. Even in the appalling circumstances of our reunion, it was wonderful to be with her again. She lived on the outskirts of Ayr, a pleasant seaside town with a fine sweep of sandy beach. I had been allotted a spare bedroom, with a camp-bed set up for Phil, overlooking the back garden. On the grass was a swing for Jan's little gold-haired Kirsty, who trotted about everywhere with a cheery freckled grin. It was very pleasing that Phil seemed from the first to find comfort in his small cousin.

We agreed the funeral would be local. Martin had few relatives to mind where he was laid to rest: we let them know, and they sent cards and regrets. I was content for Lesley to be close to Jan's family home, because they had always been so very close.

Phil and I were staying on until after the funeral, due to return home the weekend following. Malcolm's parents lived nearby — Malcolm and his father ran together a small but thriving taxi/car-hire business — and they did their best to be helpful during those strange, busy, waiting days. Faced with all the formalities, I did what I had to do, I said what I had to say. The Frasers took care of all the arrangements they could, which left Jan and me free to spend time at the hospital where tiny Lucie Marina clung to her frail thread of life. She was gaining strength day by day, one bright ray of hope amid all so much grief.

The publicity about the accident in the press and on the TV screen — it had been caused by some obstruction on the branch line — didn't help us, and we tried to shield Phil from sight or sound of it. Kay regularly forwarded my mail, including a nice letter from Hanley's telling me a representative from the Company would attend the funeral. Kay also sent personal notes making light of her problems with Richie. Myron, who rang each evening like clockwork, told me Richie's disreputable cuddly animal toy (of the uncertain species and lurid green hue) had fallen into Richie's bath and emerged several shades lighter.

On the Thursday evening, with everything ready for tomorrow's ceremony, Janine and I sat together in the quiet house. Kirsty and Phil were asleep upstairs, Malcolm was out late at the taxi office. Jan was deftly embroidering Lucie's name on a soft pink pram blanket, which we still hardly dared hope would soon be needed. I was sorting the cards from so many people who had known Lesley and Martin: among them one from John Challoner, expressing his deep sorrow. I had read it a dozen times.

In the glow of the fire we were sharing the settee by the hearth. She was so very like Lesley, the same elfin prettiness, the same eyes.

'Thelma,' she said suddenly, 'I need to speak to you, only we've been so busy. Can we talk now, about the children? . . . Well, Malcolm and I, we'd like to bring Lucie up with our own family. I was going to ask him, and then he said it by himself . . . '

'But — you have your own baby coming along?'

'Not till September. Malcolm is so good with children, and his Mum wants to help — she's a tower of strength!' She paused to look at me with sudden intensity. 'And we wondered about the boys, we'd fit them in too somehow, if — *if* you're still getting married?'

The emphasis on that small important word was striking. She rushed on, as though fearful to offend me, 'Oh, I know you're officially engaged! Only Lesley seemed to think you'd probably change your mind.'

I amended, 'She *hoped* I'd change my mind.'

'She was really worried about you,' Jan said earnestly. 'She was on the phone to me a long time while they were travelling here . . . '

'She didn't like Myron. Nor even

trust him. She made that quite plain.'

So poor Lesley hadn't waited to pour out her story. And Jan, never having set eyes on Myron, had accepted it without question. She pressed on unhappily, 'The thing is, we really would take the boys. We'd do our best for them.'

I said with deep sincerity, 'It's very good of you and Malcolm. But no, I'm not parting with them, I've made up my mind. They've lived under the same roof with me. I'm as much a second mother as they could have — or I'll try to be.'

She looked at me anxiously, plainly well primed about my foolishness in getting involved in such an unsuitable relationship but desperately afraid of hurting me.

'Don't worry, Jan! It's really nice you want poor little Lucie — you know so much more about babies than I do! I think perhaps that would please Lesley . . . '

She nodded, her lips trembling. I saw her watching the opal ring on my finger as I piled up the cards. She asked, 'But shouldn't you ask Myron about it, before you decide?'

'He'll be here tomorrow. And I shan't ask him, I shall just tell him. How about some tea?' I felt we had taken the subject as far as we could. 'Sit still, I'll make it.'

In fact, I was far less settled in my mind than I tried to appear. Not regarding my immovable decision, but for the abandonment of my own future plans. For they were by now virtually abandoned. I needed to resign myself somehow to be again just the useful Aunt Thelma, the vaguely formidable Miss Barrington who looked after other people's children. And it wasn't easy. The sunburst that broke so suddenly upon my world had left a reflection of its glory to haunt me.

I missed Myron, now we were apart. So much I missed him! — each day, all day. His smile and his voice I missed, all those little characteristics I had come to look upon with half-amused indulgence. And tomorrow would bring our reunion. Tomorrow I would know whether that bright sunburst had faded for always.

Just after I went to bed, Jan came to me with another disturbing idea. If my marriage didn't happen (or *when* it didn't, she implied) I would be left with only four walls full of memories and the lone care of Phil and Richie. So why not sell up and move within easy reach of the Fraser family? We could help each other out with all the children, we could have each other's precious companionship.

So here again my life was being handed to me neatly packaged. I promised, 'I'll think about it,' and hugged her in thanks for all her concern. Then she slipped away and left me to sleep.

Or to try to sleep.

4

As I expected, there weren't many personal mourners for the Percivals, but a huge number of flowers and messages. They came from Lesley's friends, and from many who had known Martin. His office colleagues sent their tributes, and the Department Head, Mr. Montague, duly materialised as a pleasant but remote gentleman. Martin's one close friend from work arrived with Myron.

I had met John Challoner once or twice when Martin brought him home to a meal and an evening chatting and listening to classical recordings. Always he had seemed a lonely person, serious and reserved, his dark hair quite heavily greying. I knew he was a widower with a daughter of about fourteen. On one visit during my father's illness, he talked to me about the invalid with understanding and sympathy.

I was pleased to welcome him, and tried to make him feel at home because he didn't join easily in the general conversation. But Myron, to whom the people were equally strangers, had no such problem. As soon as he arrived he was part of the family. Even Jan whispered to me, after just a few minutes, 'I do see now what you mean about him . . . '

So did I see, as I watched the mobile face that was today subdued for this unhappy occasion, that turned to me often with intimate little glances for myself alone. It was far easier to resign myself to losing him when he was many miles away.

But first there was the moving ceremony to be gone through. We left Phil with a kind neighbour who was keeping Kirsty for us. Mainly I was worried about Jan, whose tears knew no consolation. My own eyes were dry, as ever, and the words of the service, the music, the attentive faces, all were distant and dreamlike. Only when we were walking back to the waiting cars, pain suddenly broke through and the scene swirled around me.

I heard John Challoner's urgent warning, and Myron's arm was instantly around me. I had never fainted in my life.

'Better?' he said softly. 'You've been overdoing things, Jan told me how you've been helping. Now I'm going to look after you.'

'Are you?' I whispered with a kind of hopelessness. After that he kept close to me all the time. Back at the house they insisted I should lie down, and Malcolm's mother drew the curtains in my room and settled me down. I had wanted to stay with Phil, but Myron told me, 'He's fine with me, just do as you're told.'

In the quiet room some tears did come, only a few. And then came sleep. After so many wakeful days and nights I was more or less exhausted. The next thing I knew was Malcolm's mother gently touching my shoulder.

'Sorry to wake you, my dear. The

other gentleman from Hanley's left a while ago, but Mr. Challoner is just leaving — he wanted to see you before he goes.'

Downstairs there was a spread of refreshments on the table. Through the window I could see Kirsty in a little plastic cart being towed along by Phil. My head was clear again. I went into the other room with John Challoner.

'We had a little collection at the office — it's for Martin's kiddies.' He handed me an envelope. 'Please, do what you think best with it.'

'It's very kind of you all. Thank you, I'll write to them.'

'It's the least we could do.' Grave brown eyes looked into mine, and then his face relaxed a little. 'One other thing — I haven't congratulated you on your engagement. I hope you'll be very happy. I'm sure you'll never have a dull moment!'

He smiled, and I smiled back. Absurdly I wanted to delay him, to talk about Myron — because this thoughtful, perceptive man wouldn't be deluded by superficial charisma. But he was already leaving. We all shook hands, standing in the doorway: Jan had pressed him to stay overnight but he had to go back, he said, because of his young daughter Sophie. Malcolm was taking him to the station.

They urged me to eat and drink but I wanted nothing. I asked Myron quietly, 'Will you please come out for a little walk?' Jan realised my intention and whispered to me urgently to wait a while, but I shook my head.

He talked all the while we followed the road to the sea: how much he had missed me, he had checked daily on Richie, he had taken chocolates and flowers for Kay — and much more about the aftermath of the voting, his planned 'thank you' party for the helpers, and his invitations to speak in two other constituencies. His enthusiasm didn't help me.

We came out by the sea at a spread of grass with a children's playground, and in front of us an expanse of clean-washed sand and a receding tide. The sun had lost itself in leaden clouds that hung over the grey water, the cool breeze stirred the hair on my forehead. A few children were whooping on the slides and swings, but this was a long way from our brief idyllic hours recently on a southern shore.

Myron suggested, as we found a seat facing the sea, 'We could spend our honeymoon in Scotland if you like. Or do you fancy tropical sun and palm trees?'

He was holding my hand, caressing it between both of his. I sat stiff and straight.

'Before we plan any honeymoons, I've something to say.' With only that preliminary I plunged ahead. 'Jan and Malcolm are taking Lucie Marina . . . and I'm having Phil and Richie to bring up. That's a definite decision. I can manage it financially, I could always let the top flat again . . . '

My voice trailed off there. He said, 'I see,' and that was all. I waited in silence for him to speak again.

'Thelma, this is a bit shattering, I don't know what to say. Couldn't they all live here? — Jan's people seem so fond of kids. Why can't they live here?'

'She did offer, but she'll have more than enough to cope with when her own baby is born. Besides, I owe this to Lesley. And — I've already promised Phil.'

'I see,' he said again.

'I don't want to argue about it.' My voice came sharp with strain. 'I'm sorry about our engagement ... but this is something I have to do.'

'The two boys mean more to you than our marriage, is that what you're saying?'

There was silence again then. I was just waiting for the objections and persuasions that surely must come, the words he could so easily command. But he said quietly, after that long thinking pause, 'I admire moral courage. Probably because I don't have any.'

'You don't? Aren't you always ready to stand up for what you think is right?'

'It may look that way. Appearances

can be deceptive. I'm not sure I can match up to your standards — but I'll try very hard.'

I turned to look at him then, amazed by his totally unexpected response. The rare frown imprinted deeply into the young, smooth forehead aged and changed his face.

'Don't worry. We'll have that quick quiet wedding we talked about. The quicker the better now ... and yes, we'll take the kids, and bring them up to be model citizens!'

After all my hours of anxiety, how could I accept that so hasty decision? Still stern with strain I insisted, 'But you need to realise the differences it will make, I'd rather you say 'no' now than change your mind later. The worst possible thing would be if they feel they're an unwanted burden. So please give it lots more thought before — '

'No, I'd rather not think about it! Not when it means realising you expected me to walk away. That's quite an eye-opener.'

'Well, you did mention getting a little place for just the two of us,' I pointed out. 'And you don't like to be tied down, you're not keen on children at close quarters . . . '

'I did say all that, didn't I? You know, you've made me feel about two inches tall. Thelma, I promise with my hand on my heart, I won't let you down. Or let them down.'

He leant forward to look straight into my face, his dark eyes reproachful, naïve as a young child's — that most telling ploy that could sway any opposing audience. 'Darling, must you give me such a hard time? I vow solemnly I'll do my best for Phil and Richie — so aren't you even pleased?'

'Of course I am,' I whispered. In heaven's name, I thought with deep contrition, why was I being so cold and suspicious? 'It's just — I've been so worried! I'm sorry for misjudging you so badly. Truly I am.'

'Just forget it. Don't you know I'd do anything in the world for you?'

Safe in the circle of his arm, for a moment I closed my eyes, content to feel him close to me, to try to realise that after so much darkness there could still be light.

We talked then about the future. Practical as ever, I explained my ideas for the house, having the lower part redecorated, and a general rearrangement to restore the two halves to one whole. The idea of letting the top floor, if I had lived on there by myself, would hardly be necessary now.

'No mortgage, that's a boon! So don't you think we'll manage very well?'

'I hope so. Only I'm afraid I'm still a broken reed financially.'

'Still? Even after — '

'After your kind generosity.' He made one of his expressive grimaces. 'I'm glad you mentioned it, I'm not sure I'd dare bring it up otherwise. I was just wondering whether — if — you could do me one more little favour?'

'Another loan? How much this time?'

'The same as before? Or — could you possibly double it?'

For a moment I was stunned into silence. I swallowed a quite heated protest — because of what had just passed between us, my unforgivable misjudgement of him. The unwilling thought came to me, *he did know how to choose his moments?* . . . My answer sounded sharp enough, when it came at last.

'I haven't just won a roll-over lottery, you know! My Dad's savings won't last long at this rate!' There, my voice broke. So much I didn't want to be angry, to risk again our precious relationship that had just survived a near death-blow. 'Myron, I'd do anything for you too — but we can't go on this way, you can't keep wanting money without saying *why*!'

'I just don't want to bother you with miserable details. But I'll explain a bit more. Some time ago I made a mistake . . . a bad mistake, let's say the sort you don't make twice. Well, if you'll just help me pay the rest of what's owing, it'll be over with. It's nothing that can hurt you, as heaven is my witness. Can you accept that?'

'I still don't understand,' I said wearily.

'I know. But just understand one thing — I love you, with all my heart and soul . . .'

Today, how could I refuse him anything? I knew that when we returned to the house another cheque would quietly change hands.

We went on sitting there by the grey sea, talking about the future — or mainly he talked and I listened: how it would be our sacred trust to care for the orphaned children as their parents would have wished. His eloquent voice trembled with sincerity, his serious face was absorbed with purpose. One thing I had learnt today, never ever to take him for granted. The dazzling personality the world saw was merely the tip of the iceberg.

Perhaps I didn't really know him very

well. Though I drew a world of joy and comfort from his presence, did I really know him at all?

* * *

Back at the house, my first concern was to tell Jan the great problem was solved. She was delighted for me, though disappointed that I wouldn't be moving North. She said earnestly, 'I'm sure you'll be happy with him, he's really something special! I think poor Les was prejudiced over that affair of the job, or she *would* have liked him! . . .'

Which was proof that the 'Myron magic' still worked as well as ever.

We were returning to London by rail, and in the morning the Fraser family saw us off. Jan hugged me and cried, and Phil was in tears too.

But he was interested in the passing scenery, and Myron sat beside him and patiently helped to chart a list of place names to show his teacher at school. In London a Tube train clattered us through its dark labyrinth. Then came a local train, and here again was The Crescent — with the cherry blossom spent and trodden underfoot in forlorn heaps.

We had an eager welcome from Kay White, and also a lively one from Richie. Producing his favourite toy she whispered, 'Been through the washer several times — sorry it's a bit limp and faded.' I scarcely knew how to thank her for all she had done, just handing over the gifts brought back for her family.

The house was empty, so empty. The only thing to do was work as hard as possible — and there was plenty to do.

That strange Sunday was spent trying to settle in. On Monday I took Phil to school — he wanted to go or he could have stayed home longer — and had a personal word with his teacher. Following that, with Richie in the buggy I called on a local builder to ask for someone to inspect the house and give an estimate for alterations.

But still so empty the house, oh so empty! — especially through the long solitary evening. Myron rang me saying he would see me very soon, he was thinking of me, and he loved me. I knew he was due to address the Ladies Group. I imagined them sitting in a circle with cups of tea and biscuits — and speculating on what such a charming young man could see in that grim Miss Barrington.

But the following evening brought the social event I had been dreading, his 'thank you' party for the election helpers. It was my place now to be at his side. Kay White was all too willing to babysit.

The plain, dark outfit I bought for the occasion wasn't much like the flimsy dress hanging ghostlike in my wardrobe. The function was in a local hall, with refreshments and a few speeches: people were very kind, knowing the trouble I had been through. Someone was there from the local press, who wanted a picture of me alone with Myron. At least

Fred Marshall made no comment on Myron's adherence to pineapple juice.

It was a huge relief to get the occasion safely over. I had done my duty and could forget the whole thing.

And so I did forget it, during those dragging and difficult days. But it came back to me in no small way on Friday morning, when Kay waved to me as I returned from walking Phil and Jack to the school.

'Miss Barrington! — ' Still, even now, like most people she had problems with using my first name. 'I've made some coffee, would you like to come in a moment? . . .'

In her bright modern room I accepted a chair, and Richie pounced on a toy robot. The local newspaper was spread on the table: my own copy had arrived too, but there had been no chance to open it. Staring up at me were two faces, mine and Myron's close together — his smile having reproduced as well as always, my own features seeming to my eyes to be dominated by the Barrington nose.

I exclaimed, 'Good heavens above, how ghastly! It should have an X Certificate! — '

I broke off there, seeing the accompanying story. *'New Life for Orphaned Children'* announced the heading: and beneath, *'Myron Gillespie, defeated in the recent by-election but scoring a personal triumph, is next month to marry Thelma Barrington . . . . and will also become a new father to his bride's two young nephews, tragically orphaned in a rail accident in Scotland . . . 'It's the least we can do,' Mr. Gillespie told our reporter, 'to try to lessen the effect of this cruel loss on two innocent young lives . . . ''*

'I must say,' Kay commented, 'he's what your Scottish relations would call 'canny'! — People will remember this when it comes to the next lot of voting!'

It wasn't her family involved, her personal tragedy, so perhaps she didn't question this opportunity for a little free publicity. I was too shocked even to feel anger yet as she rattled on cheerfully, 'Now if that story had come out before the election, not after it — '

'Yes. Phil and Richie would have hoovered up a nice pile of extra votes for him.'

'Oh!' She looked at me with sudden disquiet. 'Well — I'm sure he meant no harm. You know, just chatting to the paper man about everything . . . '

'He needn't have brought the children in. I didn't!'

It struck me then how absurd it was having this girl defend my future husband to me. I drank my coffee and thanked her, and took Richie home — doubtless leaving her wishing she hadn't asked me in at all.

But I wasn't finished yet. Straightaway I rang a London number, to ask, 'Is Mr. Gillespie in the office this morning?' His pleasant voice was soon greeting me.

'Myron, I want to talk to you! Are you free this evening?'

'Sorry, I arranged to see the North

Ward bunch. Call-backs from canvassing, they're pathetic without having their poor little hands held . . . '

The North Ward bunch, of course, had priority. As I didn't answer he enquired, 'Is something wrong?'

'I don't quite know. I've just seen the local paper.'

'Oh, that. Didn't they do us proud? A nice booster for the public image!'

'That's what you think? If — if I'd known you were going to — '

I choked on the words. It was impossible to discuss this on the telephone. I said shortly I would be home tomorrow if he liked to come round, and then cut off the call. He could have rung me straight back. But he didn't.

Was I really being too intense and sensitive about the whole thing? Maybe by tomorrow, after more mature thought, I would take a milder view. Nevertheless, I made another phone call — to the builder, to make changes to the specification of work on the house, no longer completely eradicating Lesley's top flat kitchen. It wouldn't hurt to have it easily available for letting. Just by way of reserve.

* * *

Each of the busy days that followed seemed filled with my anxious care of the boys. When the builders moved in and turned the house into messy, dusty chaos, that didn't help at all. There were also, of course, wedding preparations, the fixed date — achieved due to a cancellation, once again illustrating Myron's uncanny ability to get what he wanted — drawing steadily closer . . . and at the back of my mind still nagging, niggling doubts and fears that obstinately wouldn't budge themselves.

Really I saw little of him. His evenings were mostly booked up, and at weekends I wouldn't leave the boys to go out, so our activities consisted of sessions in the park playground, an hour or two in the quiet house after they were in bed. Myron's restless nature wasn't content to sit passively listening to music or watching TV. Nor did he seem anxious to talk seriously at present; keeping our conversations impersonal and unproductive — and, in unguarded moments, I thought looking anxious and preoccupied.

Could he actually be regretting the decision he had made so suddenly by the grey Scottish sea? On the Saturday exactly a week before the wedding date, with Richie at last asleep after a prolonged drama, I was weary and worried enough to ask the stark question; 'Have you changed your mind?'

I had just set down a tray of coffee on the table. He stood by the window looking out at the garden, where June had touched the flower borders with colour, and toys littered the grass that badly needed a date with a mower.

'About us getting married,' I ploughed on. 'Because if you have — '

Startled, he turned to look at me.

'Miss Barrington. Madam! What sort of a rat do you take me for?'

There had been occasions, just one or two, when I might have responded, 'Well, what kind of a rat *are* you? . . . ' This wasn't one of them. I just said, 'You seem so worried, and — I wondered if — '

My voice trailed off. I was very tired, needing badly some sort of comfort and reassurance. He came across to sit beside me on the settee, and held me in his arms. I closed my eyes and clung to him.

'I've been neglecting you,' he said softly. 'Thelma, darling, I'm sorry. I thought you understood how busy I am.'

'I do understand. Of course I do.'

'It's this thing about the Stanhope Hill crossing near the school — where two little kids were in an accident recently. I'm organising a big protest next week . . . oh, but you don't want to hear about that, do you?'

'I'm interested in everything you do.'

'It'll keep, let's talk about us. You're not getting rid of me so easily. Not unless you want to?'

Indeed, I didn't want to, clinging to him all the harder. He kissed me very tenderly, while the coffee cooled unheeded on the table, the evening shadows deepened around the quiet house. My doubts and difficulties of these past days seemed to fade along with the daylight. One short week would end this hard interim of waiting.

Maybe many of our differences had been my fault — like the newspaper publicity that so angered me at the time, or our big argument over the honeymoon — my insistence it must be postponed because of the children: Phil was just tentatively settling back at school, and Richie, tiring of all the toys kind people had showered on him, clung to me with pitiful devotion when he found no tears would bring his Mummy back to him. All of that ruled out any honeymoons or holidays at present. Perhaps I had expected Myron to understand too much, too readily?

In this evening's closeness he agreed that so long as we were together it would be enough to stay home. (Nor was that due — not more than slightly? — to his current absorption in the Stanhope Hill project.)

After that evening my anxieties were less. But through that last busy week, one question stayed unanswered. If Myron hadn't regretted his decision, then what else was troubling him? Surely not the pressure of the neighbourhood's problems, for he seemed to revel in all that. Maybe his mysterious past 'mistake' — 'the sort you don't make twice'? . . . Once we were married I would ferret out the truth of that, by hook or by crook!

But on Friday I forgot all about it, because Stanhope Hill boiled up and burst through eve-of-wedding preparations. There had been another accident on that road, mercifully not too serious: not only the local paper was on to it, but the nationals got hold of the story. We had accounts of yesterday's demonstration by parents with protest banners — led by their spokesman, M. Gillespie.

Today they planned to block the traffic when the children came out of school.

Kay White told me her husband thought there might be TV people there for the local news, and would I go to watch. 'But I expect you're so busy, the day before your wedding! — what a shame!'

I didn't see it especially as a shame, too involved with last minute touches to the house, which still reeked of new paint. I had a long phone call from Jan — who was devastated that she couldn't attend tomorrow because tiny Lucie was just home from the hospital, and she herself was quite poorly. Grandma Pearson rang to tell me of course the café was being shut on the Great Day, and they would be arriving in the morning ready to help me. Myron rang twice, wanting me to record anything on the TV or radio. And another call came from John Challoner, who was leaving on holiday tomorrow but suggested calling this evening with a wedding present. I said of course he could call.

Watching the local TV news with Phil I saw glimpses of the Stanhope Hill demo, the police clearing the road by the school — Myron in the forefront objecting to being shunted on to the pavement by two burly officers

Phil, round-eyed, quavered, 'Will he get in awful trouble?'

'He can look after himself,' I assured him.

Soon after came another phone call. The affair was being included in a TV news magazine later, Myron was on his way to the studio — and would I be sure to record it.

As well as the usual bedtime struggle with Richie, tonight Phil was a problem too, still deeply worried. It was a revelation that he was becoming attached to Myron. Occasions like this, so far from the placid world of his own father, would upset him every time.

He was still awake at nine, and I brought him down by the electric fire. John's arrival with the wedding gift came as a happy diversion: we let Phil do the unpacking, and to please him plugged in the attractive table lamp and turned off the main light.

'Sorry to burst in on you,' Martin's friend apologised. 'I meant to give the lamp to Gill, but I've hardly seen him lately.'

'Join the club!' I said, and laughed. 'Do sit down, I'll get some coffee . . . and we'll all see him in a few minutes. Not to be missed on pain of death or worse!'

He laughed too. He had brought his daughter Sophie with him, a tall, thin girl with glasses and a long tail of dark hair. She sat shyly beside her father. When I returned from the kitchen I found them both discussing with Phil what he liked best at school. But the start of the TV programme upset him again.

'Don't worry, this is right up your Uncle Myron's street,' John reassured him. 'Sit here with me to watch it, Phil.'

We had some scene-setting shots of

the area and today's protest, and then the studio discussion: a bland interviewer, a group of parents, people from the Council and the School, nearby residents. After a few minutes Myron was holding the stage. The present position simply wouldn't do, bumbling officialdom or slack organisation had no place when children's lives were at stake! — perhaps your child, or my child? ... He outlined on a map possible traffic regulations and changes. He was completely at home, speaking as he might to me in this room. All too soon the programme moved on to another topic.

John asked, 'There, Phil, wasn't that good?'

'He was the best one there,' Phil whispered. 'Wasn't he?'

'He was.' John looked at me with a glimmer of amusement. 'And he didn't smile into the camera once.'

'He didn't need to,' I said.

When Phil reluctantly returned to bed, Sophie offered to sit with him. I left her softly reading aloud a favourite story. John assured me she was pleased to help.

'She hasn't many friends, she scarcely goes out unless I bully her. That's partly why I've wangled her a week off school — and also she hasn't been too well since a very bad cold in the winter ... It's one of these coach tours, everything arranged. France, Austria, Switzerland. I'm hoping it will do her a lot of good.'

It occurred to me, quite crazily, how much I would like to sit serenely in a coach in this quiet, pleasant company and watch those beautiful locations slide past. Crazy indeed! I asked, 'How old is she?'

'Almost fifteen. Her mother died when she was ten, that's when she went right into her shell — to avoid being hurt again, I suppose. She'd rather clean out our kitchen than play tennis or go to the cinema ... Sorry!' he broke off there. 'You don't want to hear all this, Miss — er — '

'Please, make it Thelma. I shan't be Miss Barrington much longer!'

'No, indeed.' He said in his thoughtful way, 'And poor Phil will have more adjusting to do! But I'm sure you'll work it out, Martin would trust you anywhere with his boys. He always thought so much of you.'

'Did he? I hope he did.'

'So does Gill. He holds you in great respect. I might say, in awe!'

My voice rose in an amazed, '*Does* he?' The kind smile that invited confidence, and my own chaotic emotions, led me to blurt out a question every bit as crazy as those thoughts about the coach trip. 'Can I ask you — do you know him well? Really know him? Oh, it sounds ridiculous, but we — we haven't been together long, it's all been a whirlwind! . . . '

He laughed, but answered very seriously. 'I think he takes everyone and everything more or less by storm. We'll all be very proud of him one day, he wants to put the world to rights — and

I admire his courage and initiative and energy. But he'll get some hard knocks along the way. He'll need someone to get him back up on his feet. Does that help at all?'

It helped so much that a lump in my throat made it hard to speak. And the lump worsened as he told me about his friendship with Martin over many years, how Martin had helped him through the time of his wife Linda's death.

The conversation was so engrossing that we forgot place and time, both of us startled when a key turned in the front door and a voice called, 'You there, Thelma?' Myron still had a key from the time I was staying with Jan. Walking straight in, he stopped short at the cosy scene he had interrupted in the dimly lighted room, the two of us side by side on the sofa, the litter of empty cups.

'Well. Pardon me, folks, I'm sure.' His smile didn't quite cover the first reaction of displeasure.

'Oh, is it really twelve o'clock?' I exclaimed. 'I had no idea, John brought us a present and we got talking — '

'So I see. Don't let me disturb you.'

Of all the emotions to arouse, perhaps the most unlikely was jealousy. If I still needed convincing of his feelings for me, I couldn't have managed it better!

John began congratulating him on the TV show, and I slipped upstairs to fetch Sophie. The boys were peacefully asleep, and she was absorbed in a book from the shelf.

There were hasty farewells as the Challoners' car drove off. Myron said he would leave too: 'Can't have my bride-to-be getting a juicy reputation along The Crescent.'

'John was telling me how his wife died, all about his daughter. All very sad.'

'While I rushed here like a lunatic thinking you were all alone.'

'Is that why you came? Wasn't it just to play back the recording several times?'

It was a shame to tease him. I saw his face was strained with exhaustion after the day's efforts and excitements. But he answered promptly, always ready for repartee, 'Then you weren't too busy with your visitor to switch it on?'

'No. And — I thought you were brilliant. Truly.'

His smile was faint and tired. I was learning how much these occasions took out of him, how a reaction always followed. I said gently, 'Thanks for coming, I'm so glad you did — but go home and sleep it all off. Or else I'll be left waiting at the church in the morning.'

'Would that bother you very much?' His eyes looked into mine, appealing in their weariness like a spent child's.

I said, 'More than very much, Myron.' I meant every word.

5

I wasn't left waiting in the morning. It was an overcast day, not much like June: but at noon, when we came out of St. Mark's — the old grey-stone church facing the Park — the sun broke through, cheering the people standing round shivering in smart frocks. I saw a background of trees, and smiling faces, and that sunlight on the weatherworn porch. I felt the strong hold of Myron's hand on mine — and Richie's hot, moist little fingers clinging all the while to my skirt, because he wouldn't be parted from me.

As we posed for photos, surely today this wouldn't be 'X Certificate' material? . . . because, laying aside troubles and griefs, I was happy. Lesley and Martin would want that.

It was touching to see Miss Baynes, in a rather amazing headgear, focussing us in her camera. Several political acquaintances were present, and the Whites, and Jan's husband Malcolm on a flying visit, and of course Myron's family. Though the affair was so low-key, it demanded some hospitality for the guests. The small reception at home was very informal, just a few refreshments and a chance to chat.

Everything was swiftly taken out of my hands because Grandma Pearson, in a sky-blue outfit straining at its seams, donned one of her café aprons and waded straight in. Her mild-mannered Fred fetched and carried. They only paused now and then to join Myron's mother, wraith-like in pale grey, to gaze in admiration at their idol.

Today I did much the same. All our differences seemed petty and trivial. He was sailing through everything with his airy grace, with the right word for everyone. I was content, happy, proud, to be at his side.

When the other guests left, and a taxi

came for Malcolm Fraser (who apologised profusely but was desperately anxious to get to the airport and home) the Pearsons took over the kitchen to clear up. Both the boys had been clinging to me as though I were a life-raft in a stormy sea: but now Myron was giving a lift home to an old lady, one of his ardent supporters, and he took them along for the ride. His mother had just swallowed three aspirins and collapsed on the sofa. After all the talk and laughter, the house was very quiet.

Grandma was busy amid clouds of steam, Fred wielding all the tea-towels I possessed. I said anxiously, 'Will Myron's Mum be all right?'

'She'll be fine. It's just made her remember her own wedding — eh, Fred?' Grandma reached for her wine-glass, parked on the window ledge, for an appreciative sip. 'It was so cruel, what happened to poor Evie. But we're really glad Myron's nicely settled down with you, Thelma. We took to you as soon as we saw you. You'll look after him, won't you?'

'Well. I'll try!'

'I said to Fred — didn't I, Fred? — he's got a streak of his father in him, it's no good denying it. Of course, Evie's spoiled him from the day he was born . . . ' (Not Evie alone, I was sure.) 'Even before he was born,' she chattered on, 'there was this film actor at the time — Myron del Maniero, a handsome devil, six feet plus and more shiny teeth than a crocodile — all the girls were drooling over him! — well, Evie's baby had to be 'Myron'. Not that 'Gillespie' had the same ring to it, and our Myron never did quite look the part . . . Shall we put these leftovers in the fridge, love?'

'Please,' I agreed. Two or three helpings of sherry had obligingly loosened her tongue enough to pour out these family confidences, now I was indeed part of that family. I prompted hopefully, 'He does look a lot like his father.'

'That's right, Rob was a real charmer . . . clever too, he could have made a name for himself like Myron's doing. But there was the drinking. He never knew when to stop. My stars, he was a wild one when he was well tanked up! . . .'

'At least Myron doesn't take after him in that?'

'You mean, he doesn't overdo the drinking? Not *now* he doesn't — and I thank the good Lord above for it, every day I do!'

'Not *now*?' I repeated.

'Oh, it was different a few years back. We were worried sick, if he'd gone the same way as Rob it would have killed Evie for sure. But he was too sensible to let it ruin his life, Thelma. All of a sudden he threw up his job and all his mates, and packed himself off North and got a room and some work — we hardly saw him, did we, Fred? . . . but he wrote regular to his Mum, he never missed. And when he came back down to London, he'd sorted himself out, bless him . . .'

I was remembering Myron relating his disturbing family troubles, in the back room at the café: and now indeed I could understand that unfortunate incident with Fred Marshall and the spilled wine on our engagement day. But as well, my thoughts lighted on an obvious link — the mysterious 'mistake you don't make twice'. Surely that fitted in somewhere? . . .

'While he was away,' Grandma rambled on, 'he spent every spare minute studying. He never did well at school, such a young scamp! — but he made up for it, passing all those exams at evening classes. And he got all these ideas about helping people and — and — '

'Taking up crusades.'

'That's it, dear. Well, we always knew he'd got a brilliant mind. And always the right words to talk to people . . . '

I was moved by her earnestness, and while she was in so voluble a mood I hoped to have learnt more. But we were interrupted by Myron arriving back, bringing the boys in to us. I saw his eyes looking from Mrs. Pearson to me with their shrewd penetration.

'What are you up to?' he asked Grandma. 'Not peddling lurid biographical secrets?'

'Not what, lovey?' she said vaguely. 'Fred, hurry up with those glasses! . . .'

We went to sit with Myron's mother, and she cheered up a little to have him beside her, her sad eyes lingering on his face. Everyone listened in awed wonder while he talked of his plans for the future. I understood better now their overflowing pride in him — because he had so narrowly escaped a very different future.

Sitting there watching, my own pride — and the warmth of my love — matched theirs. If you accepted the brilliant personality then you accepted too its weaknesses. No-one was perfect. Who was I to judge or condemn?

* * *

At five Kay called for the boys. She was to give them tea, let them play a while with Jack, then bring them back to bed and sit in until we returned from a London show — the poor substitute for a holiday at present. Phil kissed me a grave goodbye. Richie clung to me like a moist and miserable limpet.

'Poor little mite,' Grandma sympathised. 'He doesn't look well to me, Thelma.'

'He's been so upset lately,' I said doubtfully. 'Ever since . . . '

'Well, of course, poor little chap. You should bring them to stay with us a few days. A blow of sea air will perk them up!'

That didn't solve the immediate problem. I looked uncertainly at Myron. He answered by gently but firmly detaching Richie from me and handing him, a protesting bundle of arms and legs, to Kay.

'He'll be fine,' she assured me. 'Don't you worry, Mrs. Gillespie!'

There was a general laugh at my startled reaction to that address. Equally it was amazing, in my new refurbished bedroom, to see Myron's two big suitcases standing there. My reflection stared back at me in disbelief as I surveyed The Crescent and saw roses nodding brightly over garden fences. The cherry-blossom was forgotten. But I remembered it — and recalled watching it while Lesley argued, 'Surely you see it *wouldn't* work out? . . .'

We were ready to leave, and all crowded into Myron's car to drive to the Junction. I was squeezed next to Mr. Pearson, still benignly beaming. At the station we stood on the platform awaiting the Brighton train. Myron had an arm round his mother as she whispered, 'You'll phone us? — write to us? — won't you? . . .'

'Don't I always keep the Post Office service and the phone companies solvent?'

'That reminds me,' Grandma broke in, 'Fred, did you give him that letter that came yesterday?'

'No more I did.' He rummaged it from a pocket. 'Sorry, boy. So much going on.'

Myron took the envelope and looked at it. Remembrance came to me of another similar letter, when he walked abruptly away with it. This time he frowned and crushed it into his pocket. I had glimpsed the address, in cramped and ornamented handwriting: 'Mr. M. Gillespie, c/o Grandma's Cafe . . .' And in one corner, heavily under-scored, PRIVATE AND PERSONAL.

The train was approaching. There was a hasty exchange of kisses and good wishes. I stood beside him, waving until the last carriage snaked away.

After that we boarded our own service to London. In a restaurant we chose modestly from an elaborate menu: neither of us said much, or ate much. After-wards we strolled hand in hand through the summer Saturday evening streets, crowded and colourful. There were flower sellers, barrows piled with cherries and strawberries, souvenir shops hung with flags and mugs, pumping out a loud beat of music. Visitors chattered in their various languages, young couples clung together, cheery parties were bound for the lighted theatres. I couldn't recall when I last saw the Capital except purely on business.

Our theatre seats were in the front of the circle. The show was an acclaimed musical, but I was scarcely aware of anything except the man close beside me, my hand held fast in his. I was Thelma Gillespie, pledged to love him and cherish him for a lifetime.

In the first interval he peered into my face and said gently, 'You look like you need a little reviving.' He led me to a corner of the crowded bar and brought me a wineglass.

'Oh,' I protested involuntarily, 'all on my own? . . . '

'Just go ahead, don't mind me. Which leads me to ask — what was Grandma telling you in the kitchen?'

'About your father. And — '
Suddenly, perhaps rashly, I was anxious to begin our life with complete trust. 'And about you as well, how you realised in time what was happening — and worked so hard — and that's why they're so proud of you, I don't blame them! — '

'Okay. Can we drop the subject?'

'Well, you did ask. And I needed to know, you hadn't told me — '

'No, I hadn't. But now my life is an open book.'

The sharpness of his voice was startling, even making nearby heads turn. Noticing it, he made an obvious effort to smile and apologise, 'Sorry! Not the day for naughty tempers!'

Indeed, it wasn't. But I wondered, as we returned to our seats, how sketchy still was my knowledge of that 'open book' . . . and how fragile might be this bubble happiness?

After the final curtain we walked back to the station through streets alive with people and lights and bustling taxis. We didn't say much, not on the train, not in the car when we retrieved it. In The Crescent, my porch light glowed a welcome. I thought of the boys with sudden shock that this was the longest time they had been out of my mind since I had care of them.

Kay came into the hall as I opened the door. Richie had been some trouble, she admitted, but was sleeping now. She cut short my thanks, clearly anxious not to intrude. I went up to look at the children, and then changed into the beautiful deep-turquoise dressing-gown that was Lesley's last birthday gift. I unpinned my hair and brushed it out, long and loose and pale gold.

The process was interrupted by ominous sounds from the next room. I found Richie's face crumpled in misery as he squirmed and wailed. He had been very sick.

'Myron!' I called down the stairs. 'Richie isn't well! — can you bring a bucket of water and some disinfectant? — look under the kitchen sink!'

I grabbed a clean cover from Phil's bed to wrap around the shivering, sobbing child. Myron looked round the door — and commented succinctly and with deep feeling.

Phil, still half asleep, mumbled in protest, 'My Dad said people shouldn't say that.'

'Sorry, Phil. Your Uncle Myron isn't

always so polite as your Dad.'

'Could you take Richie downstairs by the fire while I clean up a bit?' I asked briskly. 'Oh, and take this potty in case it happens again . . . Phil, why not pop along to my bed?'

Blinking and bewildered, Phil wriggled on to the floor. He observed gravely to Myron, 'It's the middle of the night. You haven't gone home.'

'I haven't,' he agreed with equal gravity. 'I'm beginning to wish I had.'

I hurried to and fro salvaging poor Richie's cot, finding fresh things from the airing cupboard. On my way I changed into my old dressing-gown and screwed back the annoying floppy hair. Downstairs, surrounded by wedding cards and flowers, I found Myron sitting by the electric fire holding Richie gingerly on his knee.

He said, 'This seems to be his stock-in-trade. What does he do for an encore?'

'He can't help it. I knew he wasn't well, we shouldn't have gone out!'

'A bit late to worry about that. But

isn't the kid's face sort of blotchy?'

It was. An incipient rash was just showing.

'Chicken pox, or an infection or something,' I said dubiously. 'I'll ring Dr. Geoffreys in the morning. Thanks, I'll take Richie now . . . you might as well get some sleep, I'll have to sit up with him a while.'

'Whatever you say.' He handed Richie over with obvious relief. 'I daresay in time to come we'll laugh about this.'

'I hope so! Will you see Phil's tucked in properly?'

'Yes, ma'am.' He came across to me and gently cupped my face between his two hands. His lips on mine lingered for a long moment. 'Take that to be going on with. Despite the thorough baptism into the joys of family life — I love you.'

I whispered, 'I love you too.'

Eventually Richie was back in his cot, restless and feverish, and heartbreakingly wanting his Mummy. By now it was past three in the morning. I realised suddenly how tired I was.

Before curling up for a broken hour or two on Phil's bed, I tiptoed to the other bedroom. The landing light shone in dimly: Phil was fast asleep, but he looked still anxious. Myron was asleep too, his face young and strangely vulnerable in repose. For a long, long moment I stood watching him.

Heaven bless today's union, for me a sacred lifetime bond. Heaven grant that there should never be cause for repining and regretting . . .

Myron's jacket was hanging on the door. For an instant I was tempted, sorely tempted, to see if that strangely ominous letter was still in the pocket. But he sighed and stirred, and I slipped quietly away.

★ ★ ★

Dr. Geoffreys announced in his staccato manner, 'This young man is running quite a temperature. Keep him inside and as quiet as you can. Light diet, plenty of fluids, Miss — er — Mrs.

— er . . . How about the other boy?'

'I'll keep an eye on Phil,' I said.

So that was that. It wasn't Richie's fault, of course.

The severity of his illness was no doubt due to his very low state after all the upheavals rending his small world. At present he required much time and patience. It was hard to find anything to amuse him, to divert him from the woes of his own miserable self.

As it happened, during these fraught and busy days, Myron seemed equally engrossed in his own affairs, and was hardly at home. Stanhope Hill petered out, but other local crusades blossomed apace — an elderly lady victimised by her landlord, a retirement home denied space for a garden — and so on, and so on. Also there were meetings, post-election membership drives, and the Summer Fayre. The local paper ran an article entitled '*Young Man with a Public Conscience.*' Capping everything came an invitation to join a forthcoming television debate, *The Voice of Youth*.

I wasn't a romantic young girl expecting only moonlight and roses. We had our moments of loving closeness. There were quiet precious hours when I lay wakeful in our dim room and it was joy to me to watch the vivid, changeful face so strangely peaceful in sleep. We had all our lives ahead, so how could I resent already the ideals that absorbed him so much — when we had made our mutual bargain, he would accept and help with the boys, I would accept and help with that 'public conscience'?

Indeed, I begrudged none of his time and energy. It was only that little shadows of uncertainty still haunted me, even now, about the true depth of his feeling for me. Perhaps because I was exhausted by the fractious little invalid, my mind kept returning to one disturbing thought.

No mention had been made of the second letter he had received. I kept waiting for the subject to come up, even a request for another loan — because at least that would be a chance to settle the thing finally, for him to confide in me and trust me! But instead came a few subtle hints. The electrics on his car were possibly needing attention, but he couldn't afford it just now: I replied, grimly dispensing breakfast toast after a bad night with Richie, that he could try saving up. Another time he was sounding out my thoughts on a joint bank account. I squashed that idea flatter than any pancake.

The next day he was leaving in the normal early morning rush, kissing me briefly at the front door.

'You know I'm going straight to that meeting tonight? — oh, and can you get those notes typed up? . . . '

The usual kind of farewell. If this were indeed usual when we had been married such an absurdly short time? But as I was closing the door, he turned suddenly back. I started to ask, 'What have you forgotten?' — and then stopped. Still I wasn't proof against the pleading gaze that would melt the stoniest heart.

'I just wondered whether — ' Then

it came, as I had somehow known it would. 'I need some money. Just a loan, I'll pay it back! I did mention about the car — '

'You did. But you haven't had it fixed. Give me a garage bill and I'll pay it!'

He bit his lip, not looking at me. The lie had been clearly implied, but I was less resentful than hurt by the trouble clear in his face, by being shut out.

'Sorry,' he said abruptly. 'That was unforgivable. But — I'm a bit worried.'

He was turning away, but I reached out to hold him back.

'I know you're worried, and I want to help. But why can't you be honest with me?'

'I'll explain it later, I promise! If you could just let me have a cheque . . . ?'

Silently I shook my head. For a moment again his dark eyes met mine, now with a flare of anger. He walked away without another word. It was the first time we had ever parted in this fashion.

Wearily I went back in the house, to get through the hours until he returned. I hoped for a phone call, but he didn't ring. It was almost noon when the day's mail arrived, and then that parting scene was eclipsed in my mind.

I was upstairs when the letterbox rattled, and then there was silence — always an ominous sign with Richie around. I found him sitting on the bottom stair, busily tearing open the envelopes. Two were unimportant, and another was half open but defeating the small inquisitive fingers. It was addressed to Myron in cramped curly handwriting, one corner marked PRIVATE AND PERSONAL.

As usual I piled all the mail in a tray on the hall table. But 'out of sight' wasn't 'out of mind'. All day that letter haunted me — and the thought that in another moment Richie would have penetrated the envelope, and then I couldn't help but see the contents. The mystery had reached a stage where it threatened my relationship with Myron. This morning had been a warning.

I held out until teatime. Then, with the boys busy at the table, I picked up that letter and slipped into the kitchen. A folded sheet of paper was already visible. One tug was all that was needed.

I pulled the paper out and straightened it. It was completely blank.

Whatever unpleasant shock I had prepared for, none of my speculations had envisaged this. Its utter strangeness, almost unreality, left me completely shaken. In a way the sheer melodrama of it was typical of Myron's world. His unknown world . . .

I wished now I had left the thing alone. These were deep, dark waters.

Somehow the time passed by, seeming to last a week. When at last the boys were in their beds, I went into the front garden to tidy up dead blooms. An elderly neighbour greeted me cheerfully, 'Lovely evening! . . . That husband of yours still as busy as ever? . . .'

As the dusk deepened I went back indoors to make ready a tray of sandwiches, and then play the music that had been Martin's last gift. The haunting, swelling melody tore open the recent wounds of sorrow. Before it ended I heard Myron's car draw up.

Without a word he came straight to my chair and bent to kiss me. In the turmoil of my feelings I clung to him suddenly, almost feverishly.

He whispered, 'I've been miserable as sin all day. Please forgive me?'

I just nodded. For a few moments he talked on quite brightly about this evening's meeting, stimulated as always by contact with people and his own easy success. But then came the usual question, 'Any messages? — any mail?'

'Mrs. Chivers wants you to call round. And Miss Baynes rang — I dealt with that. And Ben Whalley to know if you'll play cricket on Sunday, South London against the North lot . . . ' As he pulled a face, reaching for a sandwich, I went on deliberately, 'Not much post — but an envelope marked PRIVATE AND PERSONAL. Well, I'm afraid Richie opened it.'

The sandwich was laid down untouched.

'At least,' I had to amend, 'Richie started it. I finished it.'

'You're very honest.' I saw the brightness fade from his face as he took the torn envelope. He pulled out the paper and turned it over, with obviously dawning relief. 'Well, that's a feeble sort of joke!'

'It's not a joke. I'm not quite that stupid. You've had two letters I know about — probably more I don't — and you admitted they're involved with your money troubles. I'd like you to tell me what's going on.'

'I'm not asking you for more money. Look, I'm really tired tonight — '

'So am I. I've been worrying all day. It needs to be settled . . . now, please?'

His eyes opened a little wider. On occasion, I was very much like my so determined father.

'Well, I suppose you'll have to know. Now she's started sending letters here . . .'

My attention latched instantly on that small word *she*.

'There's this girl, we went round together in the old days. Oh, years ago! I did live with her a short while ... Unfortunately I owe her some money. I've been paying instalments and I'm behind with them. I should have told you! — but it's not easy to confess an old flame is trying to bankrupt you! — '

'That depends on why she wants the money.'

'She helped me out once when I was in a hole. That's all the claim she has on me, I swear to you! Can you believe that?'

'I suppose so. Why did you split up?'

'Oh, she was driving me crazy. I walked out. I'm not exactly proud of any of it.'

The open sincerity of his face and voice, that had probably worked its spell already tonight on dissentients in his audience, left me groping. 'But — I still don't see — '

'I know, it doesn't explain the cloak-and-dagger bit. But you need to know Marla to understand. She's very neurotic, she gets these obsessions — she's had a lot of trouble in her life which hasn't helped.'

'Shouldn't she have some sort of treatment?'

'I've tried to persuade her, but she won't listen. She lives alone in London at present — she gets by because she had a legacy left to her. Rather like you, in fact . . .'

Rather like me. It wasn't a very comforting similarity.

'Well, I'm sorry about her,' I said briskly. 'But she can't keep bombarding you with scary envelopes! How much do you owe her?'

'I'm not quite sure — I don't quite know exactly.'

'Then will you find out? If it's not unreasonable, I'll settle it for you — no, wait!' I silenced his quick response. 'I want to be a witness when you pay it over. And you'll get a final receipt.'

'I see.' Delight and gratitude were visibly declining. 'I'm not happy about you meeting her. She gets very jealous, it could be unpleasant. I don't want you involved.'

'I *am* involved. Hundreds of pounds involved!'

'That's true,' he admitted.

'Well, I've said what you can do. It's up to you.'

Though I sounded firm and calm, I felt neither. Was that clever mind of his working apace, figuring out how much he must disclose and how much he could withhold, in order to extract the required sum? . . . Despite the warmth of the evening I was suddenly shivering.

'You're upset,' he said softly. 'I'm so sorry. I'm truly sorry.'

His arms held me, his lips were tender and pleading on mine. I wasn't proof against that — or most of all the reproach in his voice as for a moment I tried to turn my head away.

'Thelma, don't do that. Please, don't ever do that. I love you, I wouldn't hurt you for the world . . .'

'Then — just trust me. Tell me the truth.'

'I've told you. And I swear, Marla doesn't mean a thing to me, not any more. Come on, can't we forget her just for now? — I've had a hard day, can't you be kind to me? . . . '

I wanted to be kind, to believe, to forgive. Perhaps at this moment, in the persuading nearness of him, I could do all those things.

Only the cold light of morning would follow tonight.

6

Sunday was Phil's birthday, and on the Saturday morning a parcel arrived from Scotland. He stood the '*Six Today!*' card on the sideboard, and I saw his mouth quivering.

Martin and Lesley had always arranged an exciting birthday outing for him. Myron was engrossed in the morning papers, and I whispered to him, 'Can't you take Phil out with you today? Richie had such a bad night, I don't want to drag him around.'

'Phil wouldn't be interested in that wretched Garden Fete at Bill Fosdyke's place.'

'Yes, he would! He won't be any trouble.'

'Can't we just buy him something?'

'I have. He needs us to give him time and attention.'

He agreed in a slightly resigned

fashion: and then, with his customary anticipation of everyone's goodwill he added, 'I didn't have time for the car-wash, could you possibly . . . ?'

'I'm a bit busy. Ask Phil to help you!'

While I was occupied upstairs, with Richie trailing after me, I observed the scene below: the hose, a froth of bubbles, and a thrilled Phil in an old waterproof wielding a sponge. The next time I looked out, Myron was chatting to a neighbour in the sunshine, Phil contentedly polishing alone.

Well, last week the local paper had produced another snappy headline, '*Man With a Mission!*' Perhaps the mission didn't include tasks so mundane.

They went off together after an early lunch, and Richie bawled for half an hour at being left behind. Though the outing was my idea, I was uneasy. Perhaps I was over-protective towards Phil because he had been hurt so much. But in the evening he poured out accounts of his thrilling time — and how Myron had won prizes for him at every stall.

'I think he can do *anything*,' he said seriously. 'And he said I could watch him playing cricket tomorrow! — only I said I'd have to ask you first.'

I agreed of course he could go, especially as Myron had arranged he could join up with the Fosdykes' young family. On Sunday, after opening more presents, he was in a state of huge excitement. I provided him with an apple and a new story-book in case he was bored. As he climbed happily into the glistening car I whispered to Myron, 'Thank you!'

There had been a hint of restraint between us since my ultimatum of Friday night, though 'Marla' hadn't been mentioned again. Through that long Sunday, amusing Richie in the garden, I kept picturing a green cricket ground, and Myron of course making a brilliant display. Had this mysterious girl ever watched such occasions? How often had he seen her since knowing me? . . . or even since we were married? . . .

At four I went indoors to get some tea ready. Richie had a makeshift tent on the grass: the Sabbath peace was supreme, a distant plane droning, the buzz of someone's lawnmower. The house seemed gloomy and empty. Just as I went in, the phone rang.

An unfamiliar female voice asked, 'Is that Mr. Gillespie's home?'

'It is, but he's out all day. Who's calling?' It wasn't at all unusual to receive calls from Myron's many contacts, and I reached for the message pad. 'He might be out till about eight, who shall I say — ?'

'Are you his wife?'

'Yes. Can I take a message?'

There was a laugh in my ear. 'No, I don't think so. I'll give *you* a message — you need to chain him down a bit tighter. Going off and leaving you for the day already? . . . '

'Who *is* that?' I demanded, though really I knew with chilling certainty.

The only reply was the purring of an empty line.

Richie was already long asleep before the others came home. Like yesterday, Phil poured forth an excited commentary, asserting that Myron was 'the very best player in the whole match!' Despite everything, I couldn't help a glimmer of amusement. What else could you really expect?

Myron looked sunburnt, rather profusely freckled, quite content with life. He said, 'So long as you've had a good day, Phil.'

'Oh, I really have!' Phil assured him, and before going to bed thanked him solemnly for the outing. He was still too excited to sleep. With heavy eyelids at last drooping, he mumbled, 'Aunt Thelma ... I'm so *glad* you married Uncle Myron ... '

Downstairs, Myron was stretched out on the settee, and held out a hand to me. But it was easier to say what I had to say across the width of the room.

'Someone rang you this afternoon!

No name, but I can guess who it was. And I don't enjoy calls from your ex-girlfriends — always supposing they're really 'ex' . . . '

He sat up, frowning. 'That's rather uncalled for. I'm sorry if Marla was rude to you.'

'Not exactly rude. She made insinuations about you being out all day — '

'Playing very boring cricket, as you know. Another time, just put the phone down.'

'That won't fix anything, she'll keep on until she gets her money. So will you please ring her and arrange something? — or tell me where she lives so I can go myself and settle it? Suppose Phil answers the phone one day? . . . '

He got to his feet, sighing in a weary way that was unlike him.

'I'll deal with it. Leave it with me.'

With that I had to be content. He announced then he was supposed to see Mr. Weaver this weekend and it might as well be now. I wasn't to wait up. It seemed fairly clear that he went out, not for any pressing business with the Chairman on a Sunday night, but to avoid talking to me.

That night my sleep was troubled and broken. But when Janine rang me in the morning — we chatted almost every day across the miles — I tried hard to keep my private problems to myself. She was full of news about tiny Lucie, who was wondrously growing stronger. I was thrilled for them all.

News of Lucie Marina was a gleam of brightness during the days following Phil's birthday, dragging days, uncertain days. It seemed Myron was scarcely home at all — which meant at least we didn't squabble. But Wednesday was the school's Parents Evening, with the children's work on display, and he came in early to stay with the boys so I could attend. Phil's teacher told me earnestly that the child seemed wrapped up in his own world. I looked uneasily at a crayoned drawing of 'My Home', showing me as tall and beanpole thin, holding a vacuum cleaner.

The other figure, with bright orange hair, was surrounded by symbols of the boy's hero-worship — a television screen, a cricket bat, a sky-blue car.

Friday was the day of the *Voice of Youth* TV programme, to be transmitted more or less live. Phil was overjoyed when I gave him permission to stay up for at least part of it. He went off quite happily to school with Jack White and Kay.

When Myron arrived home about two, he was disinclined to talk and became immersed in some paperwork. I was upstairs when the quiet was disturbed by some loud commotion below, and ran down to find Richie on the floor, red-faced and sobbing.

Cradling the child close to me, I asked sharply, 'Did you hit him?'

'No, I didn't. I thought I was going to. He thought I was going to!'

'He's just a baby, he's been quite ill. If you can't keep your temper with him . . . ' I stopped there, relenting a little as I saw the computer print-out sheets, with columns of figures carefully highlighted and colour-coded, scribbled all over with smudgy scarlet crayon and sticky fingerprints. He began bundling the papers back in his office briefcase.

'I'll have to do the whole wretched thing again. My Home Counties sales report, I promised Old Jennings he'd have it Monday morning. It was left here two minutes while I fetched a drink. Two minutes!'

'I'm really sorry,' I said contritely. 'Look, I need some things from the supermarket — I'll drive up there with Richie and then take him to the park . . . if you can spare a few minutes to meet Phil and Jack from the school? — Phil would love that.'

He agreed without enthusiasm, still angry.

With Richie scrubbed more or less clean and fastened into his car seat, I called at Kay's to tell her there was no need to meet the boys. It was a relief to have my car roadworthy again, and the shopping was soon done. In the park I produced Richie's favourite ball. It was nice to see him well again, trotting to and fro in the sunshine. The flower-borders glowed with summer glory. Perhaps I had been shut in too much, I was too ready to blame Myron entirely for the trouble between us. And today I had so far given him no encouragement for this evening's very public appearance . . .

In this gentler mood I started homewards. The peaceful Crescent gave no sign of anything amiss. But as my key turned in the door, there came pounding footsteps, and Phil fairly hurtled into my arms, beyond coherent words.

I looked past him to Myron. He was as pale as the boy.

'What's the matter? For heaven's sake! — '

'Jack — ' Phil whispered.

'Jack? What happened to Jack?'

'There was — this motorbike . . . '

The sunshine break in the park was in another world. My blood had turned to ice.

'This lunatic came roaring round the corner — by the shops . . . ' Myron's voice was quiet and shaky. 'The kids were just going to cross, they came out behind a parked car . . . the bike missed them, thank God, but Jack fell and hit his head on the kerb . . . '

'He got taken to the hospital,' Phil burst out. 'His Mum was sort of crying. Oh, we'd waited *ages* at the school, and Jack said let's go home on our own and surprise her, so — so — '

'Haven't I told you never ever to cross roads? . . . Myron where were *you*, then?'

'I got a bit distracted. A phone call. I — forgot the time.'

For a moment I gazed at him in sheer disbelief. Instinctively I shut the front door before rounding on him.

'You stand there and tell me you *forgot*? And tonight you'll be playing up your precious 'public image', grandstanding to the cameras! — well, this shows how skin deep it is — when you

158

can't be trusted to take a five-minute walk to see two little boys safe home!'

The fierce tirade poured out. It was Phil who stopped me by bursting into tears. Myron went upstairs without a word.

'He did come for us,' Phil sobbed. 'He did! — only he was so late, and — and Miss Wilkins was talking to someone, and Jack said we could slip out while she wasn't looking . . . '

Richie, not understanding but aware I was cross and his brother upset, was sobbing too. I tried to calm them down, Phil still relating in bursts that Jack's head was bleeding, and Myron ran to bring his mother, and the ambulance man said Jack was brave.

When I could at last leave them, I made some tea very hot and strong, and put a cup and some aspirins on a tray to take upstairs. Everything was silent. I found Myron lying face down on the bed, and he didn't move or answer when I spoke.

I went across to prod him, not very

gently. 'Come on. What's done is done. Did you contact the school?'

'Of course. That stupid teacher on duty was tearing her hair out.'

'She deserves to tear it out! So do you yours! Isn't it time to get ready to leave?'

'I'm not going.'

'Of course you are. You'll be the star of the show, you wouldn't miss it for worlds!'

He lifted his head then to look at me. I was startled to see the young, bright face so stricken, his eyes actually drenched with tears. He echoed, 'Not for worlds. Not if it helps my 'precious public image'.'

'I shouldn't have said that downstairs, it didn't help. But — Jack could have been — '

'You think I don't know that? He was lying there bleeding in the gutter . . . '

He put up both hands to cover his face. Sympathy stirred within me — but also the Barrington dislike of over-emotional dramas and excessive histrionics.

'Myron, listen. You need to get a grip. Will you drink this tea?'

'Don't pretend to be kind to me. I always ruin everything I try to do — '

'Utter rubbish!' I dismissed that. 'Ask anyone about your work in the constituency — ask your boss at Hanley's, aren't you Old Jennings' golden boy?'

'That won't last long either. None of it will.'

Well I could understand his distress and remorse, but this wallowing in misery emphasised how far apart was his nature from my own. I recalled John Challoner's words, *He'll need someone to help him start over again* . . . Just now, I felt more like shaking him.

'Of course you're upset.' I was using much the same tone I might to Phil or Richie. 'It was a mistake and it had ghastly consequences. But you can't let everyone down tonight. Come on, make an effort. I'm not staying here all evening coaxing you!'

That had the effect of rousing him, at least. Anger flared hot and bright — but anger was easier to deal with.

'You've no natural feelings, have you? A block of ice where your heart should be!'

Perhaps it was as well that Phil peered round the door at this interesting moment. I took him downstairs and tried to divert his attention with some birthday toys. In a while Myron came down too — and was actually leaving the house without a word.

'Wait!' I hurried into the hall. 'Good luck! I'll be watching.'

'Suit yourself,' he said ungraciously.

Still I delayed him by putting my arms round him. After a moment of hesitation he kissed me, short and sharp.

''Bye, then. 'Bye, Phil — don't let dear Auntie throw things at the screen.'

He smiled at the boy, and Phil beamed, promising to watch every minute.

The evening seemed interminable.

But eventually, with Richie long asleep, with Phil in his dressing-gown, the long awaited titles appeared on the screen: *Voice of Youth — Teens and Twenties discuss their ideas on TODAY!*

Myron wasn't for long a background participant. With his usual vivid turn of phrase, with quick slender hands demonstrating, he had opinions, ideas, arguments, facts and figures, on every issue raised. He finished with a verbal battle against someone with opposing views, the picture fading out on him in full impassioned tide.

A rapt Phil, who had understood little of it, summed up, 'He was super!'

'He's very good at that sort of thing. Now let's get you to bed!'

He was glowing with pride and delight. As I tucked him in he asked, 'You won't be cross with him any more, will you? — Jack and me ought to have gone on waiting for him . . . ' His eagerness to take all the blame was touching.

Kay called briefly to say Jack was

staying at the hospital overnight but should be home tomorrow. I didn't know what to say to her. No one had taken the number of the motorbike, she said, as it vanished in a flash. There would be a full enquiry at the school.

Suddenly I felt for Miss Wilkins, likely to be the scapegoat. If only Richie hadn't spoiled Myron's papers . . . if only I'd gone to the school instead of taking Richie out of his way . . . if only, if only. Myron had accused me of having no feelings. It wasn't true.

I sat down to wait for him, longing for his return, my anger all used up. Because the house was so silent I put one of Martin's last gift CDs on the player. It was earlier than I expected when Myron returned. He sat down quietly and asked, 'How's Jack?'

'He'll be fine. He's staying in for observation, just till tomorrow.'

'I see. Must you play that music? — it's too sad.'

For once his resilient nature hadn't bounced back. But at least he seemed disinclined to renew our battle of wills. I said gently, 'You were brilliant tonight. You made mincemeat of that supercilious girl with the giant ear-rings . . . '

I stopped there at the sound of the telephone. He said quickly, 'I'll take it!' and grabbed up the extension from the sideboard, walking out and closing the door. Above the haunting phrases of 'Nimrod' I strained to hear his voice, and after a moment I followed him out to the hall.

' . . . Look, I've told you, Marla! . . . can't you give me a break for once? . . . '

He would instantly cut off the call when he saw me, so I made a lightning dive. I won a moment's undignified struggle, mainly because he was so taken by surprise. A voice I recognised was asking, 'Are you still there, darling? . . . '

'This is darling's wife. I believe he owes you some money — if you give me your address I'll call to settle it. And you can sign a final receipt!'

'How very businesslike, Mrs. Gillespie.' I remembered that laugh. 'Be careful, he doesn't like his women calm and efficient. He much prefers them pretty and passionate.'

I felt colour flame in my face. It was an effort to control my voice.

'Will you please tell me where you live?'

'Look in his little black book. You do have a lot to learn, don't you?'

'I'm not going to argue with you.' I drew a deep breath. 'This has gone on long enough — and we've children in the house . . . If you keep on pestering, I'll go to the police!'

It was said completely on the spur of the moment. There was an instant of silence, and then another laugh.

'I shouldn't do that, dear. I really, really, shouldn't do that . . . '

Myron ended the conversation by snatching the phone from me.

'You don't help much, do you?' I accused. 'I'm trying to get it settled for you. And I meant what I said, if she keeps on pestering — '

'No, not the police.' The sharpness of his voice startled me. 'The poor girl is sort of sick, do we want to get her in all sorts of trouble?'

'Get her in trouble — or you?'

'Thelma, I've said I'll sort it out! Just — mind your own damn business!'

He had never used that most offensive tone to me before — nor, in my hearing, to anyone else. I looked straight back into his flushed, angry face.

'All right. You won't tell me, so I'll have to take steps to find out. It *is* my business — and if it's a damned business I need to know.' I added, 'I'm going to bed, if you want any supper you can get it yourself.'

Upstairs I lay cold and sleepless, waiting, listening. The front door closed, and I heard his car start up. Then there was silence.

★ ★ ★

It was a couple of hours later when he returned, and apologised for what he called his 'stupid hissy fit'. I acknowledged the apology and then turned my face to the wall.

In the morning, it was Phil's presence that imposed normality on the Saturday breakfast table. He and Myron went over to enquire about Jack, who thankfully was doing well. Then Myron was leaving to 'make some calls' and show his face at the North Surrey Rally. In the hall where he had flamed at me, he gave me a penitent little kiss and whispered, 'Friends?'

'Friends,' I agreed, with Phil hovering nearby.

It was one thing, in the heat of last night's scene, to speak about 'taking steps'. In the cold light of morning I felt quite at a loss how to take them. Deeply I was hurt that all this trouble had been there in the background even while we planned our marriage. Equally, there was resentment against this girl who still called him 'darling' . . . and not least was the certainty that in the mix there lurked an ominous something needing to be kept clear of The Law. How else could you interpret her words yesterday?

And there was one way this jigsaw could fit together: if Marla knew something from Myron's somewhat complicated past which would scupper his hopes of a public career, might not that vague 'debt' of his be the vicious demands of a blackmailer?

Just guesswork, of course. And at this vital point my inventive powers gave out. I was still pondering it when a black car pulled up outside and there emerged a tall young girl with studious glasses. After her came a man whose hair glinted with silver in the sunlight.

The boys came running after me to the front door. I greeted John Challoner, 'What a nice surprise, do come in. — Sophie, have you grown another inch? . . . '

As they followed me through I asked about their holiday, and she answered shyly. She looked pleased that her Swiss postcard still adorned the sideboard.

Her father asked with disappointment, 'Gill isn't around?'

'He's out all day. Is it important?'

'It might be. If you could spare a few minutes to talk privately . . . '

With a chill of foreboding I sent the boys off to show Sophie the garden. 'Richie's over his illness,' I added, and gave a nervous little laugh.

The room was quiet, newspapers scattered on the table, toys strewn in one corner. On the mantelpiece stood a framed wedding photo, and I noticed John's eyes turn to that. I was remembering the last time he came to bring the lamp, and Myron surprising us. I remembered him talking about his lonely daughter.

He said now, plainly finding the words difficult, 'Please don't think I'm prying, but — is Gill in any kind of financial trouble?'

'Yes, he is.' The suggestion struck home so forcibly that I had no thought of evasion. 'I don't know any details, just that he owes some money.'

'That's apart from what he owes me, I suppose?'

'He owes *you*?'

'Oh, now I've let the cat out. I thought you knew. I told him to pay me back whenever he got sorted out . . . ' He trailed off for a moment of uneasy silence. 'Look — he's part of Martin's family now, and Martin was a good friend to me. Besides, I've always liked Gill a lot . . . in the way you can't help liking an 'enfant terrible', if you'll forgive that . . . '

I remembered the light of humour in his brown eyes. I said quietly, 'I shan't be offended at anything you say. Why do you want to see him today?'

'There's some big trouble brewing at Hanley's, I'm afraid he's mixed up in it. You see, they had a conference yesterday after he went home — I blundered in there while Old Jennings' secretary was wool-gathering — and I saw their faces and heard a few words.

And I heard his name. Old Jennings said 'I had a lot of confidence in that young man' — with emphasis on the 'had' . . . '

I might have said the same. I suggested, 'He's behind with the report he's been doing . . . but you think it's something worse, don't you?'

'I really didn't hear much, just enough to worry me. Well, I won't say any more, in case I'm wrong! — but will you warn him to mind his step with Old Jennings?'

I promised I would. It wasn't a task I relished.

John switched the conversation then to last night's TV programme and Myron's very impressive showing. I commented, 'Last night I had to bully him into even being there!'

'Don't tell me he had stage fright?'

The temptation to talk to someone so understanding was overwhelming. I intended no disloyalty, no betrayal of confidence: John had expressed his friendship and concern for Myron, he had come here especially to help him — so what could be the harm? Somehow the words began pouring out. I had worried for so many solitary hours.

After all, it wasn't so very private. The Jack White incident, the effect on Myron, a mere hint of deeper troubles I suspected. John heard me through quietly to the end.

'I suppose — something similar to Jack's accident could have happened before? That might account for the extreme reactions? Or it's just his nature, up in the dizzy heights, down in the dismal depths. Thelma, isn't that what makes him such a passionate crusader? We lesser mortals can't quite understand, don't you think?'

His kind smile soothed the sharp edges of my anxiety. I confessed, 'Quite honestly, I think I'll never understand him!' — and smiled back, in the warm comfort of his words, the reassurance of his presence. He was, I knew, a sadly bereaved man, a lonely one. People might dismiss him as sincere but slow and uninspired. Yet he carried around an aura of reasoned calm that could transfer itself in some subtle way to a troubled listener.

I was sorry the children came in then, to end these few precious moments of shared confidence. I would have liked to sit there all the morning.

7

It was in a completely spontaneous fashion that the day panned out.

Richie had been pestering Sophie to go to the corner shop for ice-cream, and she asked me shyly for permission. That led to her father offering to drive us all to the High Street, where we could choose a gift for Jack, and Sophie might get the new shoes she needed. Perhaps we could have lunch. We piled into his car, the boys well pleased that a dull Saturday was brightening up.

And for a few hours it brightened still more. In a big store we lingered around the toy section. Sophie tried on shoes, and to her everyday pair I added some sparkly-pink flipflops. Somehow I sensed she hadn't ever possessed anything like them.

For lunch we trooped into a large, crowded café. I found myself sitting at a table with Richie while the others queued and carried trays. Despite some minor upsets with Richie I enjoyed the meal quite amazingly. It was unreal to sit among the Saturday shoppers, surrounded by a chatter of voices and clatter of crockery, meeting from the man across the table a gentle, almost intimate smile — or so it seemed to my troubled mind.

Afterwards we found a wet street and clashing umbrellas. Opposite was our local cinema, its posters advertising a special Disney Matinee — *Bring The Family!*

Phil's eyes pleaded wordlessly. John asked, 'Shall we try? — if Richie gets too hyper I'll bring him out.'

Unreality was greater still. I sat close beside John in the darkness, Richie jogging on my lap then interchanging between John's and Sophie's. On hers he finally fell asleep and we watched the colourful film peacefully to the finish.

Outside it was still raining. John wouldn't hear of our waiting for a bus back, and we made a dash for his car. Phil was still in a dream of talking animals. Richie grabbed and broke Sophie's string of white beads.

Into the so familiar Crescent we turned under dripping cherry trees — that crazily seemed to me once more in their glory of blossom. Myron's car was still absent, the house silent. I insisted the visitors must come in before starting home, and laid out cookies and drinks. Eventually I tore Richie away from a new toy and finally extinguished him, tired out and angelic, in his cot.

'We'd better start back,' John said. 'Sophie's cats will be starving. Three at present, plus a one-eyed rabbit. She's a refuge for cast-off pets.'

Her serious face answered my smile, with growing confidence. I invited her upstairs and took a box from my dressing-table.

'Take this and wear it, Sophie. I've had it years but I don't really use jewellery.'

She whispered, 'Except your beautiful ring.'

'Well — that's different.' I didn't look at Myron's opals glimmering their multi-hued presence. 'Let me fasten the necklace. These beads are amber.'

'The ones Richie broke were just sort of plastic,' she protested, but I took no notice. For a moment she admired the gift in the mirror: she wasn't pretty, but they were nice dark eyes behind their glasses, her hair pulled severely back was long and glossy. I asked what she did in the school holidays, and it seemed she read a lot, tidied the house and garden, cared for her animals. As to the future, she wanted to be a nurse. Especially with children.

'You're very good with children. You cope with Richie — and he isn't the easiest!'

'He's lovely! So is our neighbour's baby, I often look after him.'

'That shows she trusts you to do it. Why not ask in your local library if there are any first-aid classes, pre-nursing

178

courses, things like that?'

Her gratitude for my interest was touching. My heart went out to the shy, too-sensitive girl who missed so deeply — despite her father's loving care — the mother who had been snatched away. Before we went down I suggested a future outing, the zoo or a picnic.

While she went out to the car with Phil, I relayed the conversation to John, and he listened quietly. The fresh cool air met us in the porch, trees still dripping, flower-heads bowed. There was the fragrance of drinking earth. The rain had just stopped.

He said, 'It's a pity I couldn't see Gill. I hope I'm making an unnecessary fuss!'

'I hope so too,' I agreed. It was unbelievable that for hours all those pressing troubles had vanished from my mind.

'And thanks for Sophie — for all today. I haven't seen her so happy since . . .'

For a moment I looked straight into

his sad eyes. And they had lost their sadness.

Not only for Sophie had today been special. We had scarcely been alone, we had talked of everyday things, amused the children, jostled through crowded shops and walked in the summer rain. But it had been enough.

The meeting eyes met and lingered. Beyond the touch of polite farewell the meeting hands linked fast. For a moment he drew me nearer to him, and nearer. I was aware of my pulses racing, my whole world becoming chaos.

The kiss didn't happen. It didn't quite happen. It happened in my heart, in my soul.

'I'm sorry.' His suddenly so familiar voice broke a silence that needed no words. 'I didn't mean to . . . '

I whispered, 'Don't be sorry.'

'Would you rather — would it be easier — if I don't come here again?'

I should have helped him, but I didn't. I stood there clinging to him, this gentle, lonely man who lived on his memories. We weren't children, we were adult people who had known loss and sorrow. We were both responsible for young lives that depended on us. Our mutual bond was acknowledged, and still unspoken was laid aside.

He repeated, 'I won't come again. But — if you need me, any time at all, let me know. If you need help, Thelma. Promise me?'

I nodded. I saw him turn quickly away to the waiting car. As he drove off, with Sophie waving at the window, just once more I heard his voice: ''Bye, Phil! . . . Goodbye — *Mrs. Gillespie* . . . '

Back in the suddenly empty house, the famous Barrington strength of will for once failed me utterly. I was moving round in a daze. When Phil was safely in bed, I started clearing up in a haphazard fashion. I was still doing it when Myron came in.

'Hi! You've had company, then?' His sharp eyes didn't miss the tray of cups on the sideboard. 'Who's been here?'

'Only John. John Challoner. He came

really to see you — '

'Then why didn't he wait for me?'

'He waited long enough. All day, more or less.'

'Very nice for you!'

'He came especially to warn you.' The last thing I wanted now was to disturb that prickly jealousy which once had seemed flattering. 'Old Jennings is gunning for you!'

'Oh? That fidgety old devil is always gunning for someone.'

'No, this is serious. John is worried about you! — and so am I — '

'How cosy. So you've had your heads together all day discussing me.'

I drew a deep breath of exasperation. 'You're impossible to talk to! Anyway, we weren't here all day, we were at the cinema!'

'Ah. Better and better.'

By now I was wholly beyond explaining about the wholly innocent children's matinee. Already I was turning to leave the room when his hand caught my arm to hold me back. He smiled straight into my eyes, that warm, appealing, sun-shine smile.

'Thelma. Darling Thelma. Must we act like a pair of moulting alley-cats?'

I said stiffly, 'Speak for yourself.' But I let him sit me down beside him on the sofa.

'I'm sorry if I upset you. I'm afraid I upset you a lot. If there's a big stink on at work I'll soon find out — but John's a morbid blighter, he likes a good worry session. Don't bother with it now, I've some thrilling news! — I've been talking to the Right Hon. Hugo Aldgate M.P. at his London flat. And Lloyd Carvell as well — he asked us both back for a drink . . . yes, *they* drank! . . . You appreciate they're our top brass? — '

'Of course I know that,' I said with grudging interest.

'Aldgate turned up at the Rally, he said he'd been wanting to meet me. There's some big publicity campaign afoot, they want me in on it. And also a by-election is pending down in the West

Country — they think I'd stand a good chance. So we could soon be moving bag and baggage to glorious Devon! . . . '

I stemmed the eager flow, 'Aren't you rather counting your chickens?'

'Oh, I'll make it all succeed! I can do it, believe me!'

Who could help but believe? It was a far cry from yesterday, when he lay flat on the bed in black despair. I watched now as excitement lighted his face, his expressive voice went on. His star was ascending again, all the brighter for its brief eclipse. He actually jumped up and pulled me to my feet to twirl me around in a joyous waltz. We collapsed back on the cushions together, laughing and gasping.

'Ssh, we'll wake the boys! . . . You're crazy, do you know that? . . . ' I started to say, and was stopped short by a ring on the doorbell.

The caller was Mrs. Chivers, a pinched little lady of advanced years who lived nearby, and had asked Myron before for advice. She apologised for calling so late: 'I just couldn't lay my head on the pillow, it's such a worry . . .'

I watched Myron usher her into the sitting room, and the sympathy and attention he gave her. When I brought her some tea it seemed he had assuaged her worries about her pension and her house repairs. She told me mistily, 'I don't know what I'd do without your wonderful husband, dear . . . you must be so proud of him . . .'

I met Myron's eyes for a moment above her worshipping white head.

He got the car out to ferry her the short distance home. After that he sat up very late in the office studying notes and figures Hugo Aldgate had given him. In the dim bedroom I lay long wakeful — and my thoughts returned again and again to one quiet promise that stood out from all of this long, long day.

'If ever you need me,' John had said. 'If ever you need help . . .'

Please God, I wouldn't need it. But

did that mean ... must that mean ... his path and mine would never cross again?

* * *

The sun shone again brightly on that Sunday morning. Myron announced he would run down to visit his family while he had a chance.

Of course, the boys were ready and eager to go too. Richie wailed on and on, 'Go seaside!' when Myron flatly refused to take him in the car. Phil supported his brother loyally, 'Uncle John let him ride in *his* car yesterday.'

We had heard a lot of 'Uncle John' during breakfast. Myron didn't comment, but his eyes narrowed. Ignoring a hint that the café would be too busy for visitors on a summery Sunday, I volunteered to take Richie on the train, a fast service from the Junction, so we could all meet at Brighton. My hope of asking Grandma more about past history seemed all too obvious.

The train was busy, but the miles slipped quickly past, the countryside was green and fresh after the rain. Richie was just becoming impossibly restless when we drew into the big station. Outside in the busy streets, with gift-shops and cafés and sunshine, there was an atmosphere of holiday. I took a taxi for a short ride, and glimpsed sparkling sea, deckchairs, tanning bodies.

The Pearsons' café was in the throes of lunches, but Grandma — red in the face, her feet oozing uncomfortably over her slippers — greeted me warmly. Mr. Pearson gave me his amiable beam. Myron was on his way by road, I explained.

'That'll cheer up his Mum,' Grandma approved. 'She's lying down. One of her 'heads'. And the dishwasher's playing up, we're in a right state! . . .'

'Can't I help? I'm good at washing up!'

'Oh no, love, you don't want to do that . . .'

I didn't want to, particularly. But

there was still that ulterior motive in my mind. With Richie safely rummaging in a basket of toys, I donned an apron and became immersed in steam and crockery. Mr. Pearson's reedy voice called orders through the connecting hatch. Grandma vibrated between her grill and her saucepans — and she chatted.

'That part-time woman who comes Sundays — never turned up today! . . . I always think it'd do Evie good to work, not lie up there brooding . . . ' She lowered her voice to a whisper. 'It's the anniversary of Rob's death, always takes her this way. — Fred, here's your burger no onions . . . '

'I suppose we all think about the past, don't we?'

'I don't hold with it, love. Thinking won't change it! But there she is, fretting herself crazy over Myron — even though there's no need any more, is there?'

'He has some big new prospects, he'll tell you about them. But — I've just been wondering — ' Intent on a stack of plates, I felt my heartbeats quickening. 'Did you ever hear of someone called — Marla?'

Suspense was prolonged because Grandpa called through to change an order, and she grumbled for a moment. But then she said abruptly, 'Marla Dalston? I never did know what Myron saw in her. Very pretty, of course. Is she still around, then?'

'I suppose he knew her before he lived — was it Leeds where he went? — '

'That's right. But he wasn't the only one, Marla had plenty of strings to her bow!' She whispered breathily in my ear again. 'We heard she had a child.'

I muttered a deeply chilled 'Oh. He didn't tell me that.'

'A baby boy, it was sick. Born sick, poor mite. Heaven knows what happened to the little kid — or to her. Why are you asking about the Dalston girl, Thelma?'

'She wrote to Myron.'

'Well, she's got a nerve! Now he's

nicely settled down with a wife and a home . . . '

There were a host more flooding questions to ask — and especially a plea on some pretext *not* to mention this to Myron. But he chose that moment to arrive via the backway, ushering a shy Phil. Grandma's face broke into a huge smile of welcome.

'You look tired, love, you've been working too hard!' And then, to my great embarrassment, 'And what's this I've been hearing about Marla Dalston, eh?'

He said quietly, 'I don't know. What have you been hearing?' He gave me one glance of deep reproach.

'You had a letter, Thelma said. I've always wondered about that poor little kid . . . '

'The letter didn't say. Thelma read all there was to read — then I tore it up.'

'Oh well, that's the best way to deal with her!' Grandma looked relieved. 'A born mischief-maker, that one. Just trying to make trouble for you . . . '

I was glad to avoid a big scene — though this was uneasy proof of how easily he could gloss over an awkward truth by a facile choice of words. He was asking now about his mother, and Grandma explained she was resting, because 'you know what today is.'

'I know,' he agreed. 'That's why I'm here. I'll go up and see her.'

'Bless him,' she murmured to me, 'he never forgets to come. Wherever he is, whatever he's doing. — Phil, come on, pet, let's find you a nice drink!'

The presence of Evie Gillespie's devoted son had such a restorative effect that presently she came downstairs, white and wan, and offered me a cold hand. The day panned out with Myron and his mother taking the children to the beach in the sunshine, while the Pearsons and I laboured in the café. But we did have a lull later, when Grandma plumped down in the back room with a box of old photographs she had taken from a locked drawer. Kept out of Evie's way, she explained, but I might like to see them.

It was strange to turn them over, with her finger pointing, her voice explaining: Myron aged six, about eight, later astride a bike. And the notorious Robert Gillespie, the huge likeness between father and son. The eyes, the smile, the flame-bright hair . . .

'That's the last one of him we had, Thelma. Here now, this is what I was looking for! That's Marla Dalston. Doesn't do her justice, though.'

I saw a younger Myron, but much as he looked now, and with him a slender, sweet-faced girl, the sweep of her blonde hair falling to her shoulders. They were holding hands.

'Don't know why I didn't throw that away,' Grandma said. I laid it back with the others. I wished she hadn't shown it to me.

Back in the kitchen we went on working. When the beach party breezed in, sunburnt and ready for tea, I announced I must start for home with Richie. Despite all the protests I set straight off to the station and a fast train.

He slept on my lap all the way. And all the way my mind revolved the new jigsaw pieces given me today, because the puzzle was beginning to fit together. It fitted too well. Nor did I realise how many more pieces would find their places until I reached home and found the house phone ringing.

Instantly I recognised the answering voice.

'He's out!' I said. 'And I warned you what I'd do if you keep pestering!'

'Yes, you'll go to the police. So what are you waiting for?' Marla's mocking voice challenged. 'You don't fancy losing your brand-new husband as soon as you've landed him, do you?'

There was a moment of silence. I spoke then very quietly.

'All right, let's come out in the open. You're blackmailing him.'

'Oh, what a horrid word! I wouldn't call it that.'

'Whatever you call it, you'll get no

more payments from us. You do know it's my money he's given you?'

'Of course,' she said, and laughed. 'Why do you think he married you? You surely didn't believe he was madly in love with you?'

Somehow I choked back a furious answer. 'Listen to me. Whatever you're holding over his head, don't you realise blackmail is a serious matter too?'

'You're wasting your time, Mrs. Gillespie. What can you prove against me? — the money has gone to charity, all anonymously to children's charities. You have children, haven't you? — two young boys? . . . I had a little boy once . . .'

I had sensed these were deep waters. I hadn't dreamt of their true murky depths. The low voice on the line suddenly was utterly chilling.

'They called your husband 'a man with a mission', didn't they? Well, I've a mission too. To make him pay for what he did. If it's the last thing I ever do . . .'

In the quiet hallway, with the big old clock ticking away the Sunday evening peace, I struggled to think. I had to decide, not only whether I could save Myron from a petty blackmailer — but whether I was morally obliged to lay bare the whole story, whatever the risk to him might be. Marla Dalston, in her confused and vindictive state, should have treatment, counselling, whatever else was necessary! There was no telling what she might do next. Her mention of my sister's precious children was a dagger of dread in my heart.

The heat of simple anger against her had almost gone. She needed help more than condemnation. So much depended on my reactions at this moment.

'I think we need to talk this over properly.' The calm of my voice surprised me. 'If Myron has really been deceiving me ever since I met him, I need to — to decide whether I'll stay with him. Will you come here to see me, or — ?'

It was that hint of a possible break-up

of our union — perhaps accidental, perhaps sheer inspiration — that gave her a clear incentive. She wouldn't resist a chance to bring that about. She said instantly, 'I'll come!'

There was no chance to arrange a day or time. The line was dead.

For a long moment I still stood there. Probably it was foolish in the extreme to invite Marla here — but I had to do something, so urgently I had to! — and might not confronting her face to face be the only answer?

There were so many conflicting responsibilities. Lesley's boys, who must at all costs be protected, even maybe sent away to Scotland until all was over: the obviously sick girl who must be stopped in her tracks before her vengeful obsession worsened: and Myron, there was Myron. Yesterday he had poured out to me all the new hopes opening up for him. Must it really be my own hand that ruined a life so full of promise, so sadly shadowed?

Perhaps it was true he married me

for my money. But there had to be more than that, he couldn't be so totally without scruple. Could I have loved such a man, even imagined I loved him? Had the light of the sunburst so blinded me?

Faint tonight was its deluding radiance. Far distant were our few golden days.

★　★　★

I didn't mention the phone call that same night. If Myron knew of the promised meeting, he would pull out every stop to prevent it, so somehow I kept the secret. Monday saw us both at the breakfast table as though this were a routine day, and then I watched him pack in his briefcase the analysis sheets Richie had ruined.

'I hope things go all right today,' I said very sincerely.

'Don't hold your breath.' His dark troubled eyes looked suddenly straight into mine. 'And promise you won't ring

Grandma to spread more alarm and despondency, they've had enough in their lives already.'

'Of course I won't do that. Myron — show Old Jennings those papers Richie spoilt! — mightn't that help?'

He shook his head as the front door closed behind him.

Phil had slept late, but with school breaking up shortly anyway he wouldn't miss much. It was well after ten o'clock when he sat spooning up cornflakes, and poured out accounts of how kind the Pearsons were to him yesterday, and Myron's Mum cried when they left, and it was so exciting driving home in the dark.

Busy vacuuming, I missed hearing a car outside. But Phil rushed to the door, and I heard him ask, 'Were you too tired to work as well? — have you got the day off too?'

'Something like that,' Myron agreed. 'Be a pal, take Richie in the garden a while?'

Phil obeyed doubtfully. He was

getting too used to high words behind inadequately shut doors. But I was determined to avoid another scene, putting the kettle on for coffee, inviting very civilly, 'Come on, then! — what happened?'

Myron sat down on my kitchen stool, not looking at me.

'You won't like what happened.'

'Well, tell me the worst. They didn't — give you notice? — '

'No notice. I'm O-U-T out. As of now.'

'But — but — ' I gazed at him aghast. 'Surely they can't *do* that?'

'They can. In the unfortunate circumstances.'

He told me just how unfortunate they were: and though I had thought myself proof against further shocks, this new twist in the M. Gillespie story was shattering. He had been dismissed, along with two other employees, because there had come to light their devious scheme to defraud the Company. It involved falsifying sales records, selling off goods and pocketing the proceeds: I didn't understand fully his confused account, just that he had uncovered the affair during his sales review and rather than report it had said nothing — for a cut of the proceeds. He had agreed to continue keeping quiet for more shares in the future. Which made him an equal participant with the others, equally guilty, equally culpable.

I exclaimed more in wonder than anything else, 'Myron, how could you be such a stupid, stupid idiot?'

'I don't know. I needed the money. I meant to pay it back somehow . . .'

'Oh yes, I've heard that tale before!' He was still steadfastly avoiding my eyes. 'So what happens next? Will you end up in court, with a criminal record?'

'They're holding another meeting, it looks like Old Jennings wants to hush it up — for old Arthur Woodruff's sake, he's been with them thirty years . . . but the Chairman wants to make an example of all of us.'

'No more than you all deserve. But in your case — apart from rights and wrongs — how could you take such a *risk*? How about Hugo Aldgate and moving to glorious Devon?'

'How about all that,' he echoed. 'Dead in the water. Thelma — if it were you, you'd resign now and be done with it, wouldn't you?'

'Yes, I would.' I frowned at his bent head, in anger, in shock, in a grudging sympathy. 'It might still be hushed up, but — '

'But these things have a way of leaking out.'

'Absolutely! And imagine how the newspapers that have been singing your praises will make a meal of it! In your place I think I'd like to jump into a deep dark hole!'

That very forcible comment at least made him look up.

'It was to pay Marla off, of course. To keep her quiet about — other things. Ironical, if you think about it.'

I didn't want to think. It was maybe

understandable that Marla's war of nerves had led him to this act so unworthy of him. But recriminations or soul-searchings wouldn't help now. I said shortly, 'Well, what's done is done. So we'll just have to live with it.'

'Shall we? I shall — but you don't have to, you don't deserve any of this. I shouldn't blame you for walking out. Or showing me the door.'

'I'm not walking out. I married you, and I'm stuck with you.' As an expression of loyalty it was so utterly blunt that even at this moment it brought a wry glimmer of amusement to his mobile face. But quickly the frown lines settled back.

'There's a committee meeting this week, what do I say to Eddie Weaver? . . . You know, all I can think of just now is the pattern of Old Jennings' carpet. I sat there by his desk and he talked to me like a Dutch uncle. I always thought he was a pompous fusspot — but he seemed really upset, he said I'd injured myself far more than the Company and

I was my own worst enemy.'

'Well, good for him. He's quite right.' Briskly I filled two coffee mugs, and offered him one. 'Come on, you've had a bad time. Drink up!'

'Why are you being so kind to me? Why not say what you really think? . . . You're a very amazing woman, do you know that?'

Was I really 'very amazing'? Was that why he had wanted to marry me? This wasn't the moment to ask.

He took one sip of the coffee and then put it down. He walked straight out to the garden. I watched him cross the lawn, his head bowed in the sunshine. I saw Phil run to him, and a small hand slip eagerly, trustingly, into his.

8

That day of drama seemed to go on for ever. It didn't get any more pleasant.

I had meant Phil should go to school after lunch, but it didn't happen. I rang with an excuse. Myron ate nothing at all. Afterwards I left him busy with the computer and loaded the boys into my car to spend a stolen spell in the park.

Arriving back, I found him mowing the neglected back lawn, virtually the first time he had attempted to share in the upkeep of the house. He remonstrated mildly with Richie for jumping straight on to his pile of cuttings, and soon had Phil busy toing and froing with a mini wheelbarrow. Viewing that idyllic scene I had much the same sense of suspicion that I often accorded Richie — whose angelic moments made you wonder what new mischief was brewing in his mind.

All the while, apart from this morning's events, the expected visit from Marla Dalston weighed upon me. Those lofty ideals about sacrificing Myron for the sake of trying to halt the girl's dangerous obsession seemed now over-dramatic, if not downright impossible.

When the boys were at last in bed, Myron went up to read Phil a story. I peeped in to see them deep in the doings of Georgie Giraffe, with Myron supplying different voices for the animal characters. He was nothing if not versatile. A ring at the door brought brief panic: *not* Marla, today of all days? ... but instead I found Miss Baynes, the vinegary Treasurer, with her usual file of papers and a certain awkwardness of manner.

Ensconsing her in the sitting room, I called Myron down. I whispered, 'I've got a feeling she knows. Like we said, secrets don't stay secrets.'

He shrugged. 'Come with me, then. Please?'

I hovered in the background as he

greeted her, 'Hi! — about Thursday's meeting, is it?' It became quickly clear that it wasn't.

Clearing her throat gruffly, she announced that as he was ignoring calls on his mobile she had rung him at work. Some 'gossipy young woman' had indicated that Myron cleared his desk and left this morning. A colleague nearby had called out audibly, 'Tell them to look out for him on Crime Watch!' — after which someone else had taken over the call.

'A friend of yours, he said. Calloway, Taberner — ?'

'Challoner,' I murmured.

'That's it. He advised me to enquire personally. He hoped the matter would be dealt with privately but it wasn't certain. I don't think it's unreasonable to ask you — '

'It's very reasonable,' Myron agreed quietly. 'If there's a criminal prosecution it'll be larceny, embezzlement, fraud . . . something along those lines. I'm sorry.'

I opened my mouth to speak and said nothing. Miss Baynes had got to her feet.

'I see. I'm sorry too, I thought perhaps I'd misunderstood. Well, I've worked for our organisation a number of years — and I'd like to say this, you were chosen for a position of trust, we supposed you were a person of integrity. I'm on my way to see the Chairman . . . '

'Of course.' Whatever Myron's feelings, he had them well under control. 'If you wait one moment I'll write Mr. Weaver a note. You can give it to him.'

Still dumbly I produced a pen, and watched him scribble a few lines. He read the last paragraph aloud: ' 'My official resignation will follow . . . this is to express my regrets and apologies and my thanks to everyone who has worked on my behalf . . . ' Will that satisfy you, Miss Baynes?'

Evidently it would. She put it in her file and left, according me a frigid 'Good night.'

I shut the door with relief. Myron said, 'Well, that's that.'

'You could have said 'personal reasons'. At least until we know what will happen.'

'I know what'll happen! Old Jennings told me to find a good lawyer, bless his heart.' He glanced restlessly at a bundle of publicity leaflets that had strayed on to the sideboard. 'And I'd better email Aldgate, stop my name going through for Devon. I'll do that now. Let the man know his all-singing all-dancing candidate is no more.'

I left him to it. The house was heavy with silence. When the phone disturbed it, again I thought of Marla, but the caller was Mr. Weaver.

'Good evening, Mrs. Gillespie.' His usual easy affability was strained. 'I'm — hem! — very sorry about — er ... I'd like to speak to Gill, if I may? ... '

I stood by while Myron spoke to him: 'Would it be best if I come round to see you? — Yes, certainly, I can come straight away . . . ' He gave a long sigh as he put down the phone.

'You didn't have to do that either,' I said. 'Not tonight.'

'Well, don't wait up for me. And — please don't bolt the door?'

'Of course not.' I groped for words. 'Myron, look — I spoke my mind this morning, I'm not taking a word back. But I think you're coping with all this very well.'

I did think that. And the wistful half-smile on his troubled face so moved me that my eyes brimmed. He saw the hint of tears I couldn't hide, and suddenly his arms enclosed me. I quavered, 'I'm sorry. I just wish — '

'What do you wish?' he prompted gently.

'How did it all go so wrong? Oh, I don't mean today, I mean — *us*? . . . '

'Us. I know. My dear, it's no fault of yours.' For a moment he held me closer. 'I'd better go, I promised the man.'

I stood alone then, unsteadily, hanging on to a chair. I heard his parting words. 'I love you, Thelma. Believe me.'

So many times I had watched him on public platforms winning his audience with that same tremble of sincerity. *'Ladies and gentlemen . . . friends . . .'*

I wasn't a public audience. I wasn't a friend.

For almost an hour I sat there thinking, thinking. It was true there was much to admire in the way he was accepting a humiliating disaster. But could there even be one strange hidden benefit in this day of downfall? — for surely it must mean Marla's hold over him was weakened, even broken? For how could she harm him more than he had already harmed himself? Threats that meant so much at the height of success mattered far less now there was little left to ruin!

As well, the carousel of my thoughts kept turning to John Challoner, imagining the furore at Hanley's this morning, his discreet voice dealing with enquiries. Was he wondering tonight how I was coping, whether he dared ring to ask? I felt a quite desperate longing to speak to him. Only, that wouldn't merely be playing with fire, but plunging into a raging furnace.

Some whimpers from Richie made me move at last. I managed to settle him without disturbing Phil, and then plodded downstairs again. I was tired by the still so new responsibility of the children . . . tired, tired by my grief for my sister and Martin . . . tired, tired, tired by the battles and disillusionments that were my relationship with Myron.

I prepared some supper for him. Set out on the table it looked very forlorn, and before I left the room I transferred a vase of garden blooms to centre the table.

In fact, I needn't have troubled. It was well past midnight when he came in, and he left it all untouched. He didn't tell me what had happened at Mr. Weaver's. He would, I supposed, when he felt able.

Through the long dark hours I was aware of him wakeful and restless.

When I rose at my usual time he was sound asleep. With Phil ready for school early, we walked the short distance in the morning sunshine, Richie in the buggy. Meekly Phil joined the arriving throng in the playground, waving to us through the railings.

As I turned away, my eyes misted once again. Poor grieving, aching little Phil. Poor bewildered baby Richie . . .

It seemed I had finally reached the point of needing quite desperately a shoulder to cry on. Stopping to sit on a bench beside a small green space, I found my mobile phone almost clambering on its own out of my bag. The familiar London office number — and then I would just say, 'Mr. Challoner in Accounts, please — it's a private call.' Hadn't he made me promise to ask for help if I needed it? Where was the harm just in a simple phone call? . . .

A voice was answering, 'Hanley's, good morning — ' I cut the call off in a sort of wild panic. I told Richie, 'Come on, let's go home.'

Surprisingly I found Myron chatting to Kay White, who was just getting in her car.

'Taking Jack for his hospital check-up,' he explained to me. 'He's okay, thank the Lord. She couldn't believe I haven't a job to go to.'

'What did you tell her?'

'Oh, that I'd had a difference with the boss. Largely true. She said there's a vacancy at her husband's place — a go-getter for the advertising section. Well, I did do a spell in advertising. Of course, I'll be stuck for a reference — but I might be able to get round it . . . Anyway, she gave me his number to ring.'

'No harm in finding out,' I said doubtfully.

'I'm just going to the Library, to look at the papers. And I've a few other things to do.' He was already turning away with a parting wave.

The long day stretched ahead. It was

impossible to settle to chores in the house: shortly I was driving off with Richie to a pleasant place a few miles distant, with a sluggish river and terraced gardens. I bought us a picnic in paper bags. But Richie was tired and grumpy, and the hands of my watch seemed weighted with lead.

It *wasn't* a good idea to idle around just thinking and thinking! — not my usual way, but this wasn't a usual me. Around two we were back at the house. There was no sign of Myron. Several messages and emails were waiting, but he could sort them out himself.

In the still pleasant sunshine I strolled to the school to collect Phil. We were right up to our gate before I realised a visitor stood by the door: at first glance a complete stranger, a slender figure in a summery dress, with loose golden-blonde hair around her shoulders.

'Sorry you had to wait,' I began, and then stopped. This was no stranger.

'Quite all right, Mrs. Gillespie. It'll

be worth waiting for.'

Cool cornflower-blue eyes surveyed me in a way none too flattering. But as she smiled, twin dimples appeared in the childlike face. It was a very attractive smile.

Ushering her through to the lounge I was chilly with apprehension. It was one thing to plan Marla's future and ours on the telephone. Face to face I dreaded to make an already impossible situation still worse.

She held out a hand to Phil, who drew back. Richie advanced doubtfully.

'You're big boys! — I've heard all about you! What are your names, then?'

'I'm Phillip Thomas Percival,' Phil stated. 'He's my brother. He's Richard.'

The last thing I wanted was for the boys to be involved with this deceptively innocent-looking stranger. Making some hasty coffee, I sent the pair of them out to the garden with biscuits and juice for a private picnic. In the quiet house I placed the coffee mugs on the table. Marla was looking curiously round the room, the sun on the pale-apple curtains, the family photographs, the china cabinet that had been my mother's.

She said almost wistfully, 'You have a nice home.'

'Yes. Well,' I plunged, 'I'm glad you came, we need to talk.'

'So you said on the phone. I'm listening! — or am I to do the talking? You want to know about your husband's dodgy past, to decide if you'll walk out on him?'

'That's right. But — things have changed a bit We've a dodgy present as well . . . ' I had made a lightning decision, a gamble indeed but it might work, it just might. 'Unfortunately Myron got involved in some trouble at work — defrauding the Company, and they threw him out. And he's giving up all his political work . . . '

I stopped there as she broke into sudden laughter. 'Miss Dalston, there's nothing funny about it,' I said sharply. 'I'm telling you because he did it for *you*! He took the money to get you and your blackmailing off his back!'

She was still chuckling. 'How careless of him to get caught. He must be slipping.'

'Don't you understand?' I flared at her, stung by that cruel merriment. 'If you want to ruin him, you've done it, you've succeeded! If that gives you any pleasure! — '

'So I'm to leave him alone now, is that it?'

'Not just for his sake, for yours too. I think you're lonely and unhappy. Why not find some sort of work you'll enjoy, a pleasant place to live — and stop brooding on the past?'

I was prepared for an angry rejection, not for the tears that flooded her bluest of eyes so soon after that pitiless laughter.

'I wanted a nice home . . . I'd have made him a nice home . . . ' She glanced at me quickly, as though ashamed of that brief softening. 'I don't need your preaching, I can do as I like!

Who's going to stop me?'

'I am. You'll get no more money. And Myron hasn't much else left to lose, has he?'

'You think so? You really think he hasn't? Just ask him, dear. Ask him! . . . '

We both gave a start then, at the sound of the front door opening. I saw Myron's face express less surprise than utter dismay. Still more I saw Marla's reaction, the joy of recognition contrasting strangely with her resolve to hurt and destroy.

He said to her sharply, 'You promised me you wouldn't come here!'

'But this is by your wife's special invitation. And I'm glad I did come,' Marla went on, with obvious glee at the look he gave me. 'She's told me you've been a naughty boy! — I'm surprised at you, I really am!'

Again he just looked at me, more in deepest reproach than anger. All my good intentions seemed far away now. The whole thing had spun out of control.

'Wasn't it kind of her?' Marla's

mocking voice prompted. 'That's how much she cares about you, darling. Such a cold, unfeeling woman. But Marla was never cold. You'd be better living with Marla. Why not just leave her to her goody-goody preaching and come home with *me*? . . . '

She had come closer to him, smiling straight into his eyes. The innocent, engaging dimples came and went. Her blonde hair was brushing his face as an arm slid round his neck and she kissed him full on the lips. He did push her away then — so forcibly that she stumbled against the table, sending the bowl of flowers flying. Somehow she regained her balance. Her voice was unnaturally quiet, as though from far away.

'You've chosen her, then. Haven't you?'

'I'm sorry. I didn't mean to hurt you — '

'You always hurt me. Well, now it's my turn. Not money any more, I'll find better ways . . . your family at Brighton . . . and your family here . . . ' She was looking straight at a photograph of Phil and Richie, her eyes hard and bright. 'Little boys upset me,' she said deliberately. 'You know why, Myron, don't you?'

She was edging to the door. I wanted to grab her back, but those last few words had paralysed me. Her final threat seemed to matter little in comparison.

'You know the first thing I can do — thanks to your dear Thelma. I'll tell your office story to the press, why not?'

She made a sudden dart out to the hall. Myron took one step after her and stopped short. The front door shut.

I whispered, 'Aren't you going after her?'

'What's the use? You can't ever reason with her.' He turned round on me with a futile flash of fury. 'You see what you've done with all your meddling? — I'd have managed her somehow if you'd left well alone!'

'I was trying to help. I really thought I could help.'

He sat down wearily on the chair she

had vacated. In lightning change of mood his voice was quiet and wistful. 'I thought I could help people . . . make their lives better . . . '

'I know.' I looked past him at that photograph, the two bright child-faces innocent and trusting. 'Myron, you heard what she said about the boys? I'll phone Jan and Malcolm, ask if they'll let them stay a while. I shan't rest till they're safely out of the way!'

He was startled by that sudden resolution. I met his eyes steadily.

'And then we'll be free to cope with Marla. She's not safe to be walking around, there's no telling what she might do. We have to do something drastic, don't we?'

'How drastic?' he asked, but he had already sensed the answer. 'You want me to make a statement to the police about her blackmail games.'

'Isn't it the only way? She'll be properly looked after — '

'She will. She'll also explain why she's been blackmailing me.'

'Can't you explain it first? I suppose — it's something serious?'

'It's serious. I daresay they can turn up their files on it.' His eyes still met mine, bright and dark in the unnaturally pale face. 'Do you realise you're asking me to walk straight into a prison sentence?'

'Oh, you can't know that! — can you?'

'I've always known. I should never have married you without telling you, it was — unforgivable . . .'

He was visibly shaking, and his face was more ghastly grey than white. Something made me hold out my arms, as I might to a troubled Phil, and clasp him close to me.

'It's all a nightmare — but you're not alone. We'll get through all this somehow . . .'

There were footsteps clattering through from the garden, and I saw Phil's face light up at the sight of his Uncle. Myron looked at me over the boy's unsuspecting head.

'If I don't do what you want, am I to understand you'll do it for me?'

I couldn't answer that more than impossible question. In haste I left the room, to make my so urgent phone call across the miles to Scotland.

9

''Georgie Giraffe's Big Adventure'. Again.' Myron made a wry face, after reading Phil his bedtime story. 'I nearly dropped off before he did. Did you ring your sister?'

It was the first time we had been alone all evening. He sat down by the window to look out at the garden where yesterday he worked so hard. The flower-borders were tranquil in the late sunlight. It was a beautiful evening. This was a beautiful summer.

'Yes, I just said we had some problems — and they'll have the boys to stay, but not right away.' I spoke with all the anxiety I felt. 'Jan needs some hospital tests this week. I hope to take them at the weekend.'

'I see. Well, you're probably right to worry about them — and Marla too. Which doesn't leave me much choice, does it?'

'Oh, I wish there was another way! Suppose I explain about Marla to my doctor? — or we can try Social Services — or Citizens Advice — '

'Whatever we try, the first thing she'll do is blurt out the whole sordid story. You know, I used to think, if I could do some good in the world it might balance things up a bit. But you can't wipe things out that way. Even if you spend your life trying . . . '

'I still don't know what your sordid story is, do I? Did you have a few drinks too many and rob a bank? — trick an old lady out of her life savings? — '

'You think I'm capable of both, don't you? Well, you're right about the drinks. But — but . . . ' He trailed off with almost a shudder. 'I don't think I can tell you now in cold blood. Tomorrow I'll screw my courage up somehow and hand myself in — and then you'll know what sort of individual you were tricked into marrying. But — it'll kill my poor Mum . . . '

I had already thought of the home at

Brighton, the loving family. I tried to say gently, 'Your Mum will get over it in time, whatever happens.'

'Will she? Grandma is a tough old bird — and Grandpa will stop smiling for a moment and then put some more burgers on the grill. Mum is different. And so are you. Can I ask you something? — when you take the boys to your sister, why not stay there? Find somewhere nice to live, start a whole new life? — a much happier one, I hope. We — can get our marriage ended. Heaven knows you've plenty of reason to end it . . . '

Even now I wasn't prepared for the wide-open emotion that recalled vividly the aftermath of Jack White's accident. He hid his face in both hands, a lock of his copper-bright hair falling over them.

'I promised you so much, didn't I? And I knew I couldn't give it to you. I led you on into thinking you loved me . . . '

Those last words struck deepest of all. Had I ever truly loved him, had it been all some insubstantial dream? — the springtime visions of awakening new life, a new joy, a whole new sunlit world? At this moment of disillusion warring with instinctive loyalty, could I find it in my heart to love him still?

His voice went on, quietly, painfully. 'I married you — well, largely for mercenary reasons, which was cruel. But since then I've come to respect you and admire you more than anyone I've ever known. I love you now, Thelma, very much. With all my heart and soul I love you . . . '

A timely ring at the door saved me having to find an answer when I had no answer to give. Old Mrs. Chivers greeted me eagerly as I struggled to speak to her in a normal way.

'I'm sorry, Myron isn't very well tonight. Is it something urgent?'

It wasn't. She just wanted to tell him her insurance problem was settled due to his help. When he came up behind me, she looked at him in concern.

'My dear, you look like a ghost!

You've been overdoing all your good work.' She reached out and patted his arm. 'Make sure you look after him, Mrs. Gillespie! . . . '

For a few minutes more she exuded gratitude, until her final farewell: 'Good night, my dears, God bless you.'

'And you,' Myron said. He shut the door, looking at me with a kind of helplessness.

'Poor innocent old duck. I can't stand much more of this — I'd better go out now, tonight, and say my mea culpa to the authorities.'

'No, not tonight. You're tired and upset, you'll need a clear head. In the morning I'll go with you.'

'I don't want you going with me!' His voice rose in sudden passion. 'I don't want you involved! — and that's why you should just move right away with the kids! . . . '

'Come on, let's try to simmer down.' I attempted to calm him much as I might curb Richie spotting an ice-cream shop. 'Maybe you're taking too much for granted. Whatever tales Marla can tell, there mightn't be any proof . . . '

'Proof?' he repeated. 'He died, didn't he? Isn't that enough proof?'

I echoed the word, *'Died?* . . .' It seemed all my blood turned to ice.

We were still in the familiar hallway, with the brass umbrella-stand glimmering, the tall old clock ticking ponderously. I slumped down on the stairs because my legs wouldn't hold me. I whispered, 'What are you saying? . . . who died? . . . '

'You imagined something like that wretched office thing. But there was a life involved. You can see why I couldn't bear to tell you.' All at once we had changed roles, he was the more composed.

'But — it wasn't deliberate! — '

'Marla thinks so. She told a lot of lies to cover up for me.'

'I don't care what she thinks, I'll never believe that! Just — just *tell* me!'

'It isn't easy to tell — because even at the time I didn't really know what happened. I'd had a lot to drink, I should never in a million years have been driving . . . '

'You had an accident?'

'Worse than that.' The low voice went on beside me. 'There was a big outcry in the media about a hit-and-run driver who left a child dying by the roadside. Well, it was Marla's child. A few months old. She kept following me, waylaying me — we had terrible fights but I couldn't get rid of her . . . and I was driving back quite late, and there she was again, in the rain and the dark, waving at me to stop. And I must have gone crazy, she says I drove straight at her. I don't know if I meant to. I don't know . . . '

I was beyond words. There had been so many heights and depths, and I hadn't given way. But it seemed now my strength had all ebbed away.

'So — she was knocked flying but not much hurt — but she was holding the baby, he was flung in the gutter. I slowed up and looked back, I saw him there . . . and I didn't stop, I just drove

on, because I was scared out of my wits
— if I had any wits . . . And he died,
he'd hardly had a life at all. I got away
with it because she described a different
car and a different driver. We've both
lived with it ever since. I think of it
every hour of every day. I dream of it at
night . . . every night, every day, all the
time . . . '

He was so good with words. Far too
good.

'If I'd had the courage to stop,' his
anguished voice still went on, 'if he'd
got to the hospital — he might have
lived. But all his little life ran away in
the gutter with the rain . . . '

'Stop it!' I burst out at last. 'I don't
want to hear any more!'

'There isn't much more. The only
thing that kept me sane was working,
working and trying to achieve something worthwhile. And I didn't hear of
Marla for a bit, she was seeing someone
else but it didn't work out . . . and then
this last year, when things started going
well for me, she turned up again. She

wanted money to keep her mouth shut — more and more, all I'd got and all I could borrow. That's why I got involved in the swindle at Hanson's. And all the time she *still* wanted us to be together, that was the alternative to blackmail and ruin. I couldn't do it! I couldn't face spending my life with her!'

'Even though she had your child?'

'He wasn't my child!' he said sharply. 'He was a poor little sickly wailing thing . . . he wasn't mine! Thelma, I'm ashamed to say this is another reason I married you, I thought it would finally drive Marla away. And — if not, you did have some money in the bank . . . '

He trailed off there. I knew now — dear heaven above, I knew! — all that lay behind the engaging smile that had promised me a life in the sunshine. I understood the secret guilt that drove him to unsparing devotion to all his crusades and causes. Indeed, it wasn't his fault that he had found pleasure in using his own aptitudes. Yet all the while something of the hidden pain had added to his impassioned words, his instinct for reaching the anxious and stricken, bringing to their eyes the tears I had thought so weakly emotional in his own.

They were mine now that brimmed over. I so seldom cried but I was conscious of tears streaming down my face, almost wondering where they came from. I heard his voice again, close beside me.

'I don't know what to say to you. I'm desperately sorry, but that won't help. I just don't want you to be hurt any more . . . '

'I don't think I *can* be hurt any more.' The words were a sob. 'You're not really going to walk into the police station tomorrow with this horrible story?'

'Marla will do it, sooner or later. Didn't you recommend getting in first?'

'I didn't know then, I didn't dream! . . . Will they call it 'death from dangerous driving' — or surely not manslaughter, or — '

He shrugged his shoulders. 'Any name will do. And if Marla can get me one extra day behind prison bars, she'll call it the justice of heaven. She's probably right. I did what I did. Come on,' he urged gently, 'you're trembling, will you go upstairs and lie down? — '

He tried to help me up. His fingers were ice-cold. It was then that I turned on the stairs — and saw gazing at us through the landing railing a pair of horrified eyes in a small pale face. Whatever Phil had heard or understood, it had been enough to transform him to a silent statue of horror.

★ ★ ★

Upstairs in the dim bedroom, where Richie was sleeping in blissful unawareness, Phil's bed was tumbled, the story book Myron had read for him still lying there. All I could do was cradle the child close to me, repeating again and again that whatever happened, he and Richie and I would always be together.

Vaguely I heard footsteps below to and fro, Myron's voice on the telephone. Phil was just a little calmer when the footsteps came upstairs, with an accompanying chink of crockery. Myron brought in a tray of steaming mugs.

'Look what we've got, Phil,' I whispered. 'Hot chocolate, your favourite!'

There was a dim lamp in the room kept alight for Richie. By its glow I hoisted Phil up. He was shivering despite the warmth of the summer night. I whispered to Myron, 'Who was on the phone?'

'Oh, two newspapers trying to confirm a story. Marla's been busy already.' He turned to Phil with a very fair attempt at his usual manner. 'Come on, cheer up! Didn't Aunt Thelma tell you you'll soon be going to your Aunt Jan's at the seaside?'

Phil quavered, 'I don't want to go without you coming.'

'You won't need me, you'll have lots

of people! And perhaps I'll follow on later.'

'No, you won't. I know why, I heard.' I was to learn that beneath Phil's shyness lurked a goodly strain of the Barrington character. 'I heard what you said, you're going to get in awful trouble — you'll be in — in . . . 'cos you manslaughtered someone . . . '

Myron's eyes met mine as he commented, 'You're a remarkable family for getting down to the bare bones of a situation.'

I gave Phil an unconvincing assurance that he mustn't worry, everything would work out somehow. But our voices had at last roused Richie. He announced with satisfaction, 'Mornin'. Get up now!'

'No, you're not,' I hastened to crush that idea. 'It's still night-time.'

He had spotted Phil's mug of chocolate. 'Want a dwink. He's got a dwink.'

Pouring a little into the spouted beaker thoughtfully provided on the tray, I looked round at Myron.

'I'd better stay in here tonight while Phil's so upset. Could you fetch me some pillows and a blanket?'

'Yes, ma'am,' he said meekly.

For ten minutes there was a bustle of basic domestic activity. Just as I finished constructing a makeshift couch, Richie neatly flipped the lid off his beaker, turning his surroundings a soggy brown. Myron was leaning silently against the door watching me, his pale face strangely wistful.

'I can sort this out. Why not try to get some sleep?'

'Yes, ma'am,' he agreed more meekly still.

I dropped what I was doing to follow him on to the landing. He whispered with clear distress, 'Will Phil be all right? I didn't want the poor kid to be so worried . . . '

'Well, you're — a sort of hero to him.' I could speak calmly now, because the everyday tasks had rescued me from as near hysteria as I had ever known. 'I'm sorry I went to pieces. I'm over it now. And tomorrow I'll leave the boys with Kay — or whoever I can get — and come with you. I might be able to help a bit. I just want to help.'

'Do you? I've tried to persuade you not to stay here. Remember that.' He put out a hand to me and then uncertainly drew it back. 'I'm truly sorry. I don't know what else to say. Tell me you can forgive me, even if you don't mean it . . . please? . . . '

There was still that compelling appeal in the dark troubled eyes looking straight into mine. For a moment I could say nothing because his lips were warmly, urgently on mine. 'I forgive you,' I gasped out at last. And then, because I couldn't face any more emotional scenes tonight, I added a gruff 'Goodnight!'

He echoed, 'Goodnight.' He glanced back at me to say it again — only this time it was 'Goodbye.' The significance of the changed word didn't strike me at that moment.

Before fitful snatches of sleep came

to me, there were glimmers of daylight in the sky. It was a car starting up in the early hush of The Crescent that disturbed me: I looked drowsily round the room where the boys were both sleeping, and last night seemed impossible — except for a tray of cups, this uneasy bed of mine on the carpet.

The house was silent as I slipped from the room. The bedroom door was ajar: I looked round it hoping Myron might be sleeping. But the bed was disarranged and empty, there were drawers askew, signs of hasty packing. I fled downstairs and all the rooms were empty. A piece of paper on the kitchen floor, perhaps wafted from the table, was scribbled in familiar handwriting:

Dearest Thelma — I couldn't go through with it. Sorry to let you down again. Love you.

His name was signed with its usual flourish, contrasting with the message that must have been wrung from hours of solitary conflict.

Bitterly now I blamed myself for my absence of foresight, remembering the intensity of his parting last night. Even then, was a plan stirring in his agile mind? Perhaps to slip away and so avoid me sharing his dramatic mission this morning? Perhaps to plead with Marla again for an end to her vendetta — or to promise their lives could be shared as she wanted? Perhaps simply to run away from the task he had set himself?

I had steeled myself to support him through today's ordeal, but now I had no idea what to do. Almost an hour was wasted in hoping he would just come back. But he didn't come back. Again and again I tried ringing his mobile, leaving messages that varied from a stern *Don't play games with me, this isn't fair!* to a pleading *Myron, please ring me, please tell me where you are, what you're going to do* . . .

When the morning papers arrived I glimpsed a photograph, an adjoining paragraph about 'a promising new-comer'. I tossed the whole bundle down in the hall. Very soon after, the phone rang — but it wasn't Myron's voice.

'Sorry, Mr. Weaver, he's out. And I don't know when he'll be back!'

Sharp disappointment made me unduly abrupt. He coughed in obvious disbelief. He was anxious to minimise damage to our local image, he didn't know how these stories had leaked out but if I were approached would I refer back to him. I agreed almost without interest, because the local image seemed at this moment of small importance.

After that the doorbell sounded. This time it was the vinegary Miss Baynes, newspaper in hand. I repeated wearily, 'He's not here, I've no idea when he'll be home.'

She too was incredulous — as well as immensely indignant. She seemed to feel that as Myron had been obliged to resign, he had spitefully leaked the story in order to complicate matters for his successor.

'That's rubbish!' I flared at her. 'I do know who spread the story around . . . ' How could I start telling a far-fetched tale of pathological revenge? 'But I can't explain just now.'

'I see. There's one more thing, your husband had cash from the funds for some extra leaflets, we haven't seen any sign of them yet — '

The fierceness of my own reply startled me. 'Send me the details, you'll have payment by return! And I'm not prepared to listen to any more of your accusations!' I closed the door in her affronted face.

At least now a plan of action was forming in my mind. I spotted Kay White opposite watering her pot-plants, and my signals brought her rather doubtfully across the road.

Along The Crescent people were leaving for work. There were bright flowers in their gardens. This was just a normal day.

'Sorry, Kay, but I have to go out — and I wondered — '

'Oh! Well, I'll be out too. I can't help with the kids today.' She dropped her voice to a whisper. 'We just saw in the paper . . . Harry is going ballistic!'

I asked stupidly, 'Why?'

'Why? — he recommended Myron for the job vacancy, he spoke personally to the Manager. It's made him look a complete clot!'

Picturing her tall, stern-faced Harry, some years older than his lively wife, I felt I very much didn't want to meet him.

'Please tell him we're very sorry. And it really doesn't matter about the boys.'

She suggested if I popped in when Harry had left, we might fix something. I believed it was mainly interest in the lurid details. But it was good of her even to be civil, after Jack's injury and Harry's embarrassment.

Back indoors, Phil was looking round for me. I reassured him, 'I was just talking to Jack's Mum. And Uncle Myron went out.' Quickly I decided on the best approach. 'He didn't tell me where, so we must find out — and I'll need your help.'

He agreed to that eagerly. We went upstairs to root out Richie, who was in a fractious mood after his broken night. There followed a more than usually stressful breakfast episode. I slipped aside to make another phone call.

'No, love.' Grandma Pearson's voice was breathless and surprised. 'We haven't seen him. What's the matter then, Thelma?'

Evidently they hadn't seen any newspapers either. I told a vague tale about Myron losing his job and disappearing, and she clicked her tongue indignantly.

'Walked out on you, did he? And left you with those kiddies, worrying your heart out! If he comes here I'll ring you — and I'll give him a piece of my mind! . . . But there you are, he's his Dad's son . . . take a lot of living with, the whole bunch of 'em . . .'

I pictured her rushing to tell the mild and inarticulate Fred. Doubtless it would send Evie Gillespie straight to bed with one of her 'heads'.

Prominently on the kitchen table, among uncleared breakfast debris, I left a note to say where we were. With Richie in the buggy and Phil beside me I made for the High Street: there again was strange normality, people shopping and chatting, buses rolling by. Further on was the turning with the solid brick bulk of our local Police Station. I held fast to Phil's cold hand.

At the counter I asked whether Myron had called in, explaining he had possibly intended calling with a personal problem. He hadn't called yet. I gave my name and address and mobile number. Back in the street I was conscious of complete anti-climax. I could have done more than this! I *should* have done more! . . .

We checked in vain the car-park at the railway station. Back in the house, my scribbled note was untouched.

We had been home perhaps five minutes when the doorbell rang, and

Phil and I both made a dash. In the porch was a tall pleasant-faced man who I recognised before he handed me his card: a certain Tom Gates from the local Gazette. He was simply doing his job. It was unfair of me to shut the door almost in his face.

A moment later, the phone rang. That was merely a wrong number.

It was a combination of all this, and Phil mournfully surveying Myron's coat hanging in the hall, that brought me to a new decision. I picked up the phone again 'Hanley's, good morning,' a girl's bored voice responded.

'Could I please speak to Mr. Challoner? This is Mrs. Gillespie — it's very urgent! — '

I heard someone whispering and giggling. It no longer mattered.

Another voice said, 'Thelma?'

$\star \quad \star \quad \star$

Foolishly I stammered, 'I'm sorry to bother you when you're busy — '

'No, I'm glad you rang, I've been so worried about you. How is he? — I saw him on Monday after Old Jennings had done with him, he didn't look good.'

'No, he wasn't good — but he'd have come to terms with it, we'd have managed. It's something different now, something much worse! And last night I persuaded him to report it all to the police, but — he's just vanished and I don't know what to do, he just *won't* answer his phone — *why* won't he answer his phone? . . . I've tried everything, and I've got the boys here — and they're involved too, and his family at Brighton . . . '

There was a moment of complete silence after that very incoherent explanation, until John said quietly, 'Try not to worry about him too much, he's — well, unpredictable, impetuous — but he's a survivor. But as for the children and the family, that sounds serious. Can you wait for an hour? I can be with you in an hour.'

'Can you really come?'

'Of course I'll come. And I'll get Sophie over right away — she'll help with the children. Will you be all right till we get to you?'

It was only a few days since I last saw him. Since we agreed he wouldn't come to my home again.

The time of waiting seemed endless. Everywhere in the house, there was Myron, talking to me, smiling at me. Just as I settled the boys with milk and cookie 'elevenses', the doorbell sent Phil flying into the hall. His excitement quickly became disappointment.

'Still no news?' John asked me, and I shook my head. 'All right, would it be best if you tell me the whole thing from the start?'

I switched on a TV children's channel. Out of range of the boys, I talked while I made coffee. John occupied the stool Myron used on Monday to tell me about Hanley's. I stumbled through the story of Marla, with no scruples now about disclosing confidences.

'Here's the note he left. And, John, I

just thought — I don't believe he has any money, so what will he do? — '

He took the paper with obvious reluctance, read and returned it.

'They have to be found. Both of them. We can't have him getting into more trouble with some crazy idea — nor let this girl wander at large with her obsession of revenge. It could get a bit too dangerous.'

I whispered, 'I know. If anything bad happens it'll be my fault for dithering.'

'No, not your fault. He got himself into this unholy mess. You've tried your best — but now it's time to pass things on. That's what we have to do.'

I nodded, absorbing confidence and comfort from that gentle, steady voice. Then I heard Phil jump up again as the doorbell rang once more. John greeted the new arrival briskly, 'Sophie, you've made it! — well done, you're just in time.'

Whatever reasons he had given her for this sudden summons, she was plainly full of eagerness to help. Her father explained we would like her to stay with the boys a while and monitor any calls. It was only a moment later, while I was finding my bag and coat, when that benighted telephone trilled again and she grabbed it quickly.

'Mrs. Gillespie, it's — somebody Aldgate?' she whispered.

'I can't talk to him. Whoever rings, please take a number, say we'll ring later.'

A short while ago a call from Sir Hugo would have had Myron up in the heights.

I produced a meaningless 'Don't worry!' for Phil as I left the house. Outside the sun had just pushed through early clouds to light damp pavements and refreshed leaves. I felt John's hand gently hold my arm.

'People just keep on ringing and calling, they're like vultures!' I said shakily. As if to prove it, Kay's door opened and she signalled to me, with a speculating glance at John. She asked if I had made other arrangements for the boys.

But the small delay was providential. Phil rushed out, in wild relief to see us still nearby: he shouted for all The Crescent — or all the world — to hear, 'Auntie, he's at the café! — so now you needn't go to the police again!'

Whatever people heard, or thought they heard, didn't matter.

Grandma's familiar hard breathing down the phone line greeted me, 'That you, love? Well, he's here! Just walked in as large as life.'

Relief and anger churned within me. 'Thank you. Can I speak to him?'

'Of course! And — look, don't be too hard on him, eh? He's very upset.'

That was the Mrs. Pearson who earlier had uttered castigations on the whole Gillespie family. Plainly I heard her side of a conversation in that distant room: 'Myron, she's waiting! — talk to the poor girl, she's been frantic about you! — '

She came back to me, for once at a loss. 'Sorry, my dear, he just won't.'

'Never mind! I'm on my way, I'm

leaving now! Grandma, don't let him leave — knock him on the head, lock him in, just keep him there!'

At least the waiting was over. There were a few minutes of brisk discussion: John hadn't his car, as he had come from London by train: I had mine — but experience of driving Richie to the coast wasn't encouraging, and a fast train calling only at Gatwick en route would be quicker and easier. We could scarcely leave Sophie here alone with the boys for unspecified hours to come.

So all of us set off together. At the Junction there was a mad dash for a train just leaving, and we caught it by a hair's breadth. Richie, suddenly aware we were bound for the seaside, wriggled gleefully around on Sophie's lap to see from the window. Even Phil looked less anxious now. Opposite them, next to John, I was vaguely aware of the miles slipping past, people in summery clothes, Airport travellers with assorted luggage.

'This won't take long.' John's voice was soft and close. 'Then at least you'll be able to sort things out with Myron.'

'Yes, he has a lot to sort out,' I said with unusual bitterness. 'A public scandal, all his work ended — probably prison — a breakdown for his Mum . . . and a divorce for us.' I felt without seeing his eyes intent on my face. 'That's what he wants me to agree to. And I'm to set up home near my sister in Scotland. Well, they did suggest that, after Lesley died . . . '

'I see. May I ask how you feel about all that?'

'I don't know. We've been together such a short time. He had — his own reasons for marrying me . . . and I've found out the man I loved so much never really existed.' My voice was a soft wail of pain. 'It was a marriage of false pretences. Does that make sense? . . . '

'It makes sense. Very sad sense.' For a moment there was just the gliding motion of the train, his hand on my arm. 'There's something I was going to say to you. Perhaps this is the right time. Do you remember I mentioned my sister June — who married an Australian engineer, they've three kids now, they're happily settled down . . . '

'She wanted you to go out there too?'

'After Linda died she kept pressing me about it. Well, she tells me there's the likelihood of an accounts post in her husband's company for someone with my experience and qualifications. It's probably true Sophie needs a complete change — she's too lonely and introspective, the three little cousins would make a new life for her. So — for her sake . . . '

There was nothing I could say. I just waited.

'And for us too. You and me. I never dreamed there might be anyone else in my life after Linda. But now — you see, with you not being free, this might be a good thing to do.'

Only too well, I saw his meaning. He was virtually waving me goodbye.

'I'm really inclined to go ahead. I've talked it over with Sophie.' He paused, his brown serious eyes looking straight into mine. 'But at present I'm still not committed.'

'So you're saddling *me* with a decision like that! — it's not fair!' I burst out half angrily, and then came quick remorse. His words had amounted to an open declaration of his feelings for me — and it was in my power to respond, to accept the future he offered. Hadn't Myron himself implored me not to sacrifice the rest of my life to an undeserved loyalty? 'I'm sorry,' I tried to say, 'I do understand, but — '

'But I'm taking too much for granted?'

I shook my head. I had known him really so little, but our thoughts and our minds, our two grieving hearts, were in accord. I knew how desperately hard a permanent parting would be for both of us. And how impossible would be any future contact between us — if I chose to stay with Myron.

'Thelma, let me just tell you this. Whether we went there together or stayed here together, I'd do anything to give you happiness — to make a home for you, and my Sophie and your boys. Anything in the world.'

His eyes still meeting mine were filled with their warmth, their gentle humour, openly now their love. This was the second golden vision that was being offered to me within a year of time. Could Phil and Richie ever hope to find a father-substitute more sincerely caring, more understanding of their bereaved little lives? . . .

'Of course,' he was saying softly, 'you can't decide anything now. But — will you think about it, when you can?'

'Yes. Yes, I'll think. But I have to say — I made my marriage vows truly believing I'd keep them.'

'I know that. I know *you*. I promise not to mention this again unless you want to talk about it. And I won't tell my sister anything just yet.'

His hand clasped mine and held fast. I clung to him. I closed my eyes upon the children's faces, the green country-side slipping past.

10

The sea-front was busy. There were lines of traffic, summer-clad people around the shops and cafés or baking their well-oiled tans a shade darker. On such a day, I remembered, the exclusive Miss Barrington once rested too upon a sunny beach listening to the wash of the tide, building a mirage on a kiss.

The taxi from the station made short work of the distance to a street where another shop or two displayed their wares — and a painted board advised passers-by to *Try Grandma Pearson's Home Cooking*. No-one was trying it just now. The door was shut, its gingham curtains pulled across.

At the rear was parked a pale-blue open-top car.

I rapped on the kitchen door. There was a debris of partly prepared meals and a pervading smell of something burnt or burning. Grandma sat by the littered table, her bulky form slumped in a chair. The mild little Fred was patting her shoulder, offering a steaming mug of tea.

'Is he still here?' I asked without preliminary.

For once it was Fred who answered. 'Upstairs, Thelma. With his Mum.'

There seemed no adequate words of relief. I nodded, and turned to beckon to John and Sophie, discreetly hanging back with the children. Friends who had been helping, I told Mr. Pearson. In the midst of it Grandma suddenly roused to instruct him, 'Fred, give them anything they fancy in the café, something nice for the kiddies!'

Phil was reluctant to go, but John took his hand to coax him along. Mr. Pearson, in his long blue apron, his bright-eyed crumpled face curiously unchanged, ushered them through the dividing doorway. I took his place beside Grandma's chair.

'Sorry, love.' She blew her nose

forcefully. 'Myron's been telling us. It just knocked me in a heap.'

'I know what you mean. I was the same last night.'

'Of course, we've always worried because he's so like his father. Charm birds off their boughs one minute, and then the next . . . But we thought he was doing so well . . . ' She made an effort to steady her voice. 'Look, lovey, he told us about the money he's had from you. We've got a bit put by, Fred and me. We'll pay you back the money.'

'Please, I don't want it! That's the least part of it!'

'Well, we feel responsible. He's treated you bad.' She set her mug on the table, huddling back in her chair. Before this I had never really thought of her age, but all at once she looked an old woman. 'Poor Evie had such hopes for him. She'll worry herself sick, that's something else he'll have on his conscience! . . . '

She lifted her head then abruptly.

Both of us heard a door shut some-where above, a creak on the staircase. My heart suddenly was racing.

'Well, how is she now?' Grandma said.

That unmistakable voice answered, 'She's still lying down.'

'I'll go up to her.' She hauled herself out of her chair. 'You talk to Thelma, after she's rushed down here. That's more than you deserve from her!'

The door shut behind her. I looked across the littered kitchen and was suddenly startled to see the face so young, so appealing, even just a shadow of that ever-magnetic smile in greeting. He said simply, 'Hello.'

'Just 'hello'? — is that all? When you went swanning off into the blue, didn't you stop to think what you were leaving me with?' I found myself flaring at him. 'The papers, the neighbours, Hugo Aldgate — Miss Baynes hinting you'd dipped into the funds! — '

'Sorry. I did guess what you'd be facing. I thought it might be the last straw — you'd think 'oh, to hell with him!' and start packing a bag.'

'Oh.' It wasn't the first time the workings of his mind had amazed me. 'Well, I didn't, I moved heaven and earth to find you. We asked at the police station — '

He made one of his expressive grimaces. 'I did go there, first thing — and drove straight past. If I'd had the courage of a wet lettuce I'd still be there.'

Suddenly I understood the rending solitary battle he had fought and was still fighting. If I didn't love him as I once thought, still I cared deeply about his ruined life, his shadowed future. From the bottom of my heart I cared. I said very quietly, 'All right, we'll forget all that. Just be straight with me. What are you going to do now?'

'Oh, you know me — always full of bright ideas. I've collected Marla from her flat and driven her down here. She's waiting for me on a seat by the sea with a packet of sandwiches. Cheese and pickle sandwiches . . . You see, I felt I must see my folks to tell them the truth in person, it didn't seem right to let them hear it secondhand . . . '

I nodded, appreciating the massive resolution that had needed.

'I hinted to Marla that I'd split up with you. She thinks she's staying here with me overnight in a hotel, and tomorrow we're off on holiday. Not exactly true, of course.' Again there was just a ghost of a smile. 'I'll meet her at three, and once she's in the car I'll zoom straight to the police station and rush her in before she has time to protest. Nor any chance to get at my family and your boys. Poor Marla . . . '

Now, even now, he spoke of her still with genuine compassion. I agreed, 'That sounds a good idea.'

'Well, that's plan A. There was also a B — just to lose her in the crowd and shoot off to Gatwick to hop on a plane, a plane anywhere! And send the confession details on afterwards. Only that would need money. I wanted to ask Mum for it just now — but I couldn't ask her for the money to run away, I couldn't do it . . . ' There was a break in his voice. 'And I'm not asking you, either — so plan B bites the dust.'

'Good.' I could scarcely control my own voice. 'Stick with plan A. And you know I'll go with you if you want.'

'No, you could help far more by staying with Mum. She'll need a lot of comforting. And so will you — isn't that why you've brought John Challoner along? . . . I was watching from upstairs when you arrived, I saw you two together. It told me quite a lot.'

'John's going away,' I blurted out. 'To his relatives in Australia!'

'Is he, indeed. Well, you don't have to part company. You could go too!'

'He's already asked me. Are you a mind reader or something?'

'Or something. I saw what I saw. Good for him! — you'll regret it if you say no.'

Whichever course I took would bring regrets. It was a question beyond answering. It was a choice impossible.

In the café area, Richie was messily immersed in strawberry jelly, Sophie patiently assisting. Phil, his bowl untouched, jumped eagerly to his feet.

'Hi there, Phil,' Myron said gently. 'How about going down on the beach?'

'If — if you come too?'

'I'm a bit busy. But Uncle John will take you if you ask him nicely.' He looked round at John and held out a hand. 'Greetings, friend. Good of you to come along.'

John shook hands, awkwardly clearing his throat. 'I'm — er — so sorry about . . .'

'I know. Look, that money I owe you — Grandad will square it with you.'

'Please, just forget it. I didn't really expect to see it again. Is there anything at all I can do to help you?' John asked quietly.

'Yes, one very big thing!' Myron stood looking up straight into the face of the taller man, deeply serious.

'Thelma told me your plans for Australia, you're a dark horse and good luck to you! I've been trying to persuade her she needs new horizons too. What a perfect answer this would be for her and the kids . . . '

The composed presence of John Challoner was thrown suddenly and utterly awry. He stuttered and stammered unintelligibly — and I shared his embarrassment.

'I mean it,' Myron went steadily on. 'I admit I haven't been exactly ecstatic about you two. And heaven knows I don't want to lose Thelma, she means all the world to me . . . but there's precious little recompense I can give her except this. Well, come on, say something, mate! Can't you see I'm pleading your case for you?'

'I think Thelma will make up her own mind when she's ready,' John said stiffly. 'I've told her I won't try to influence her decision.'

'Of course you won't! The pair of you are too civilised for your own good.

And Thelma is as obstinate as a whole train of mules . . . Perhaps she'll listen to you, tell her what sort of sentence I'm facing. Something fairly grim, yes?'

'Well.' John cleared his throat yet again. 'Er — I'm afraid . . . '

'I'm afraid so too. During which time, you can be a happy family across the globe — with my blessing, for what that's worth. Good sense, John?'

John mumbled quite desperately, that he was being placed in an impossible position.

For me, nothing was real any more. I heard Myron say he mustn't keep Marla waiting or she might get suspicious. And then there was a sound on the stairs, and I saw the stricken tearless face of Evelyn Gillespie. Grandma was still blowing her nose loudly.

'Let's just get this over,' Myron said.

He embraced his mother. Grandma enveloped him in a bear hug and subsided again into her handkerchief. Old Mr. Pearson, the meek little man usually just part of the background, said quite steadily, 'P'raps if I came with you, boy? — a bit of moral support?'

'I have to do it alone, Grandad. But — thanks.'

I shook my head at Myron not to speak to Phil again. Richie had set up a monotonous clamour, 'Want to go in *tar* . . . wide in blue *tar* . . . ' Sophie was trying vainly to shush him.

'May I, Thelma?' Myron came close to me and kissed me, his lips on mine warm and tender. Lastly he extended a hand again to John, with a parting whisper, 'Look after her.'

I didn't go out to the yard, though the others did. In the empty room I held tightly to Phil. It seemed there was a commotion outside, someone crying out — Myron's mother, I thought: the disturbance lasted a few rending minutes and then the car drove off in something of a rush.

When they all came in, Grandma sat Evie down with a mug of tea and instructions to pull herself together, and then waded straight into clearing the muddle left from the café's sudden closure. She called to Fred, 'Don't stand there gawping when there's work to do!'

For the moment I couldn't help them. The walls were stifling me. I slipped out to the yard, deserted in the sunshine, the gates still open where Myron had driven out. Mechanically I shut and fastened them. I looked along the street, down a turning that gave a glimpse of sparkling sea.

There was no need for heart-searchings, for weighing and balancing. I knew what I must do. Thelma Barrington had always been so good at making decisions: and now Thelma Gillespie, breathing in the relieving fresh breeze, also knew her mind.

'Are you all right?' a quiet voice asked behind me.

I looked at John and tried to smile, but I was visibly shaking. He came closer and his reassuring arm was round me. I stood stiff and cold.

'I'm just going in to help Grandma . . . but first I must tell you . . . John, your sister can start making arrangements — for *two* people. Just you and Sophie.'

For a moment he didn't speak. The longing to respond to the gentle encircling arm was almost overwhelming. He said at last, 'Shouldn't you give yourself more time? It's all happened very suddenly.'

I didn't need time, not any at all. This was instinct, not reason. Because I was so tired and shaky I found myself leaning my head against his shoulder, his arm clasping me more closely. I whispered, 'Oh, how can I make you understand . . . '

'I do understand. You have to do what you think right. But must you decide now, today — without even waiting to see how Myron gets on?'

'Whatever happens, he'll need someone. Very badly. He was just putting on an act in there, just for his family. Oh, I'm not making any excuses for him, but he's been paying for what he did ever since — he's tried to make some amends in his own way but it's always been there. Now he's finally stopped running away from it . . . ' I stumbled over the words. 'He says he tricked me into marrying him, in a way he did — but I'm not a child, I had my eyes wide open. And I can't desert him now. I'm very, very sorry.'

'I see. Well, I admire your courage — and his too. I shouldn't have barged in and made things even more difficult, I should have — minded my own business.'

'Please, don't say that! Don't ever feel like that! I'm so glad I've known you . . . you and Sophie . . . and if things had been different — '

He nodded. He never wasted words. I read in the sad brown eyes that looked into mine, suddenly as eloquent as Myron's ever were, a depth of feeling that matched my own. I turned away, because I was very close to breaking down.

On the paving at my feet something

was lying, and I picked it up. It was a spoon smeared with red jelly. Richie must have dropped it when he was with the others watching Myron leave.

I said, 'Where did Richie go? He's very quiet.'

'I don't know. Sophie is looking after Phil, we thought you had Richie.'

'I haven't seen him. Not since — he was wanting a ride in Myron's car . . . '

A quick disquiet came into John's face. I followed him inside, and for a few moments we searched and called. It was very quickly obvious that Richie wasn't there.

★ ★ ★

It was possible the child had slipped out through the left-open back gate. Also it was possible he had stowed away in Myron's car: it wasn't beyond his resourceful powers to take advantage of the chaotic scene of departure — everyone busy with Evie's hysteria — and curl up small behind the front seats. If

Myron failed to notice his passenger at first glance, he was in no frame of mind to look more closely.

'Myron will come back here when he finds the little kid, Thelma,' Grandma suggested doubtfully. 'He will, won't he?'

'He might not find him until he collects Marla — and if there's a big scene Richie might just stay hidden. Oh, but he could have just wandered off down the road — '

'We'll all look. He can't have gone far,' John tried to reassure me. 'Let's split up and search. You've tried Gill's mobile?'

'Of course! It's switched off. How can he be so *stupid* . . . ?'

In the street Fred and John and Sophie all joined the increasingly frantic search. Among people and shops and sunshine, no small solitary figure was anywhere on the pavements. I doubted anyway that Richie would do this, because since Jack White's motorbike incident he had been scared of streets and traffic.

But still I was scurrying and peering up and down when John met up with me. He had at least something to report: he had phoned the local police, and Myron and Marla hadn't yet presented themselves, either with or without a stowaway. John had explained as well about a young child going missing.

I was grateful for having the basic organising taken out of my hands. Those deeply emotional moments with John such a short while ago, that had seemed to tear my world apart — or what was left of my world — were totally unreal.

He believed the best plan was to go to the spot near the Pier entrance area where the meeting between Myron and Marla was to take place. We might find them still there — or maybe even meet the car on its way back with Richie. It sounded good sense. This was a big, big place to comb for a small, small child.

A while ago I had felt exhausted, but

that was past and gone. I clung to John's hand that had quietly taken mine, and linked like teenagers we threaded through dawdling people, running, constantly looking around. There were cars, other cars. There were children, other children. In the dazzle and glare of the sea-front, families were on the beach, sun-worshippers draped in their deckchairs.

'No sign of them.' John was breathless but still coherent. 'Sure this is the place?'

'This is what he said! Oh, I'll ask someone! — somebody might know . . .'

Maybe I hadn't made it plain enough to him that Marla Dalston — who had so tragically borne and lost a son — nursed now in her mind a morbid fixation against small boys, and I had seen her cool eyes lingering on my sister's children. Indeed, was it not to save any risk to them that Myron had accepted the ruin of his life? Yet now it seemed helpless little Richie could actually be face to face with her. I dared not let my imagination wander.

'Excuse me!' I hailed a whole row of semi-somnolent chair occupants. 'Has anyone seen a man and a child? — it's very important! A little boy in a yellow tee-shirt with a blue duck on the front . . . and they were meeting a very pretty girl with long blonde hair . . . '

It seemed a hopeless question in that busy spot. But there was a quick response.

'Yes, we saw them — didn't we, Frank? . . . ' A bulky grey-haired woman prodded her husband. 'A man with red hair? — that's right, tell you why we noticed them,' she rambled on with infuriating slowness, 'she was sitting here waiting and the young fellow came along holding the boy's hand, and they started the very devil of a row! Embarrassing, it was, we didn't know where to look! And their little boy got out of sight on the beach, they were both down there looking for him — '

'Did they find him? Did they?'

'The girl did, she came up the steps

carrying him. And a bit later the young man rushed up and asked which way they'd gone. Well, it *was* a bit odd — '

'Which way? Did you see which way?'

'Over there.' She pointed a hand.

'Thank you! Listen he's not their little boy, he's mine! — and the police know he's missing, will you tell them all this if they come here?'

I didn't wait for comments and questions from the line of deckchairs that had all sprung to interested life. I clung to John again as we dashed across the road. The street the woman had pointed out was lined mainly by hotels, the nearest standing back behind a paved parking area where a few cars stood. One of them was a familiar sky-blue.

We made a dive between passing traffic, making an irate driver shout at us. Myron had plainly left the car in great haste, half by a 'Staff Only' notice and half in a flowerbed. At that same moment, almost under the wheels of another apoplectic driver, he was running towards us, flushed and breathless — and alone.

'You haven't found them?' I jerked out at him, and he answered just as tersely, 'No! — but they were here just now. Hop in the car!'

Hastily John explained our side of things. Myron said he had found Richie huddled behind the seats, half camouflaged by scattered newspapers: he called himself every sort of fool for not spotting him as he left the café. In the haste to escape that emotional scene, it was forgivable.

I still muttered, 'Why didn't you phone when you'd found him?'

'I meant to bring him straight back to you, didn't I? — I tried to explain to Marla, but she thought it was some sort of trap, we had an unholy row! . . . '

We knew about the unholy row. There was no need or time for more words. I found myself sitting beside Myron, as I had done so many times, his familiar voice very close.

'I saw them along here, but while I was dumping the car they vanished. — John, will you take my phone, ring Grandma to let her know? — the number's in here . . . ' He tossed back his phone. 'Marla might have dodged in a doorway but if we keep touring up and down . . . she can't have gone far walking the kid or carrying him . . . '

'When you saw them,' I whispered, 'was Richie — ?'

'He was fine. She was holding him.'

'But — what will she do with him?'

He said expressively, 'God knows.' He was cruising slowly along the street, with all our eyes scanning every doorway and entrance. He added quietly, 'I'm not sure she knows herself. The trouble is — her child was called Richard too. That's worried me all along.'

'Myron, you never told me that — ' I tried to say, and my voice gave out.

'I know. I didn't want you to know.'

Yet another secret he had kept, yet one more — and now this revelation pierced me like physical pain. I forced myself to stay silent, to keep searching the street, almost willing my eyes to see a bewildered little figure in a yellow tee-shirt. But it was Myron who first exclaimed, 'Look there!'

At first it wasn't Richie I saw, nor was it Marla. People were standing on the pavement, staring upwards, exclaiming, pointing. Passing vehicles were pulling up.

Myron lurched the car to a halt. This was quite an impressive mansion of a hotel in red brick ornamented with stonework, one arched window probably lighting the main staircase. Above that, at the highest storey, a stone ledge ran around the building. On that ledge the breeze was fanning out the snow-white dress of a golden-haired girl as she edged along inch by perilous inch. One arm gripped a small child who was clinging round her neck. There was no need to see the child's face.

How she had reached that lofty perch — from a window or balcony, aided by convenient water pipes or sun-blinds — didn't matter. My instant impulse was to rush to the hotel entrance, but hands held me back, both John's and Myron's.

'Don't let her see you! Do you hear me?' Myron hissed at me.

'But — I have to do something, I have to try — '

'No! Just this once, do as I say! — please! Please!'

'The fire and rescue people?' John was muttering.

'Yes, make sure they've been called — and keep Thelma right out of sight! If Marla will listen to anyone she'll listen to me, I'm sure I can get Richie away from her. She's doing this just to frighten me . . . and oh boy, is she succeeding!'

I heard my own voice wail, 'You'll all be killed! All of you!'

'Shush. She can't hold the kid like that for long — I'll have to rush.'

John offered, 'Shall I come? — can I help?'

'No, it'll only scare her. Just stay with Thelma. Just — spare me a little prayer? . . . '

Then he was gone. My dazzled eyes strained upwards into the sunshine. As I crouched low in a bed of shrubs, the heavy scent of flowers all around, John called softly after him, 'Be careful, Gill!' Pointless advice, it seemed, looking at that dizzy height, that narrow ledge.

I was oblivious to surrounding onlookers, shocked comments, heads and faces at windows. Despite every warning, almost it was impossible simply to wait and watch. I was aware of John beside me, holding me still, whispering 'There's help on the way . . . '

But every second was a lifetime — and the approach of rescuers might so well cause Marla to panic. I was going to say that, but the words froze suddenly as I saw Myron at an open window high above. It even seemed I could hear him speaking: I couldn't make out the words — but the voice that could engage a crowded hall would be soft and intimate now, for Marla alone. Gentle so she wouldn't be alarmed, pleading so she might co-operate . . .

He was on the ledge, moving towards her. Slowly, almost casually it seemed, little by little. All the time he talked to her, holding her attention. I saw her face turned to him, the sun on her beautiful hair. I saw my sister's beloved baby son, too petrified with fear to cry.

Only once the child struggled, trying to reach Myron — and the movement almost overbalanced the girl who held him. There was a gasp of horror from the watchers below, a great sigh as somehow she recovered. Still Myron was entreating her, with as much apparent calm as though they were down here among the flower-beds. I prayed silently, if ever his gift for persuasion worked, let it work now! Please, dear God, let it work! . . .

With those waiting moments an unbearable eternity, I had to close my straining eyes — and it was another sigh, and the pressure of John's hand on my arm, that made me open them. Seeming to cling to the brickwork by the force of some unseen magnet, Myron reached out to take the terrified child. His hand touched Richie, gently and insistently he disengaged the clinging little hands from Marla. It was the most dangerous moment of all. It needed not merely supreme courage, but as well no little physical strength.

But wasn't this the man who always had loved to play to the gallery? — so at this public moment how could he fail to give the performance of his life? The perilous transfer was made, the weight of Richie was held by his own encircling arm. Now clearly I could hear the boy's sobs. There were waiting faces and hands at the window to receive him — but it was a long way back along the ledge. A few feet were like a mile.

A gust of relief came from the watchers as those eager hands at last pulled Richie to safety. The child vanished through the opening. There were still hands extended — but Myron was shaking his head, refusing their help. He turned back along that accursed ledge.

I had half risen to run to the building, to reach Richie. John held me firmly back.

Marla had moved too, further along the narrow pathway. At the corner of the building an exuberant stone-mason had blossomed it out into a sort of ornamental turret, possibly a niche to carve the date of construction. As she reached it, one foot slipped and she almost fell. Someone near me screamed aloud.

Slowly and surely Myron followed her. He reached the corner, he was very close to her. His protecting arm went around her. He was still talking to her. I thought I could even sense the words: 'We'll stay here very still . . . we *won't* look down . . . '

Marla did look down. After that stumble it seemed her nerve was gone. She clawed at the wall, trying to wriggle from his sustaining grasp. Again she slipped — and this time it wasn't one foot but both feet. For an instant it was just Myron's hand that held her. She hung from his grasp like some helpless puppet dangling on a broken string.

The strain was too great. His numbed fingers weakened, there was an appalling instant of struggle. She fell like a stone.

And the great jerk of her falling displaced Myron's hold. He had lost his footing, clinging to the stone turret with deadened hands. Too late there were people on the roof with ropes, voices shouting 'Hold on!' — and the approaching sirens of racing vehicles.

I heard his unforgettable scream of terror, that froze the horrified watchers as they ran forward to where Marla lay. I saw him fall, striking some jutting stonework and hopelessly clinging and clawing, slithering ever downwards, the final impact as he landed.

Although others were nearer I was the first to reach him. I spared one glance of pity for Marla, her white dress spread around her where she lay.

'Don't try to touch him,' John warned, still beside me.

I wasn't trying, just looking at the face quiet and still and unmarked. Almost without understanding I saw the flood of a deeper crimson that was drenching that ever-flamboyant hair. Then his eyes flickered open, startlingly bright and dark, looking straight into mine and lighting with pleased recognition. He said distinctly, 'Hi! . . . is Richie . . . ?'

'He's safe. You saved him, he's quite safe.'

'But poor Marla . . . I couldn't hold her any more, I tried . . . I did try . . . '

'Of course you did, you were wonderful. There's help almost here, so don't worry about anything,' The words came out with almost my accustomed brusqueness. 'Just stay very still. Don't try to talk!'

'You were always such a bully.' Uncannily there was a vivid flash of his smile. His voice was quite strong. In dismay I feared his senses were wandering as he began in the old familiar way, 'Ladies and gentlemen . . . friends . . . '

'Myron, don't,' I whispered. But he wasn't wandering.

'We've had too many words — and words are cheap — so I'll leave you with this thought . . . you can say of M. Gillespie — he died better than he lived . . . '

Again there was just a ghost of that smile. The dark eyes closed on the blackness of their pain. But after a moment one hand moved weakly, pushing away a coat someone was spreading over him. He murmured, 'Thelma, you're too far away . . . '

'I'm here, darling. I'm here,' I whispered.

The ambulance was nosing on to the forecourt. I clasped the groping hand between both my own.

'Hold on to me . . . hold me . . . I'm frightened . . . ' His breath caught in a gasp and the hand gripped mine. 'Keep holding me . . . '

I kept holding, every moment that I could. There were faces and movements around, us, ministering hands, skilful hands, all unreal and dreamlike. Soon there was the speeding vehicle with its urgent siren, the entrance to a big building. I held on until he was whisked away from me, lost in the closed-in world of the hospital.

Then I sat in a soulless room, with some tea untouched beside me. until one of the busy doctors came to tell me, grave-faced, what I already knew.

The exuberant spark was quenched, the restless mind was at rest. At twenty-five Myron had left behind his chequered world, its dazzle of brilliance, its torment of trouble.

I said, 'Thank you, that's what I thought.'

My eyes were dry. The weight of grief and loss still was scarcely understood.

There had been no chance even to tell him my decision to remain with him into the future, whatever it might hold. Now it was too late. Now he would never know.

11

'He didn't let my brother fall off. He saved him, didn't he?' Phil kept saying again and again. 'But why *did* that lady take Richie up on the roof?'

'The poor lady was sick. Sometimes — when people are ill — they do strange things,' I tried to tell him.

Late into the balmy evening following that almost endless day, I held his hand in a bedroom above the café. He had been told a watered-down version of the tragedy — because it was best that he heard it from us. It seemed that so often I had shared with Phil these moments of grief.

But thankfully it did make some difference that his new idol had left us in a bright blaze of glory. It served to erase from his mind those bewildering doubts and fears about Myron that recently so worried him.

Tonight I could only give thanks that Richie was safely back with us here, of course shocked and exhausted but virtually unharmed. John and Sophie had gone with him to the hospital after the rescue, but later we were all driven back together.

It was a huge relief to find Myron's family already knew the details. Grandma carried Richie straight upstairs and laid him to sleep in her own bed, sitting beside him and softly crooning to him. Long after the child was asleep, she still sat there silently weeping.

It was a relief too that for Evie Gillespie, as for Phil, Myron's last spectacular act of courage was something to keep her afloat in the floods of grief — almost as though she could more easily bear her adored son dying a hero than living on with public disgrace. Now all those wicked things could never be proved, she kept murmuring. We left her with those sustaining thoughts.

For myself, I knew what I must do. I

had promised Myron to stay for a while with his family. Grandma had already prepared this room — Myron's old room — for me with a camp bed set up for Phil, and tomorrow she could borrow a cot. I would need to travel home briefly to collect some things, to make some calls, but it was too late that same night. The Pearsons wanted John and Sophie to stay too, but I pressed John just to take his daughter straight back home. They could be there before midnight.

'Please? — Sophie needs her own bed, and her animals . . . to be away from all this . . . '

Of course, there would be people to see, arrangements to be made, questions to answer and ask: John and old Mr. Pearson — the old man proving amazingly strong again in this desperate emergency — had already phoned Jan and Malcolm for me, and taken care of the beginnings of all the rest. In the following days we would be more than busy, with official enquiries, the press not abandoning quickly a tragic human story . . .

John asked me quietly, 'Will you be all right? Are you sure?'

I would be, I said. I had the boys, I had Myron's family. Already Fred was phoning for a taxi to drop the tearful Sophie and her father at the station.

It was a brief parting. I said, 'Goodbye, I can't thank you enough for . . .'

John shook his head to silence me. Just for an instant his hand touched mine.

That was all. A lifetime ago were those moments when his arms held me close to him. A lifetime ago my rejection that tore apart his dream and mine, all his painful regrets for blundering into a crumbling marriage that was 'none of his business.'

I was truly grateful now for his help on this appalling day. Just grateful.

I made a few phone calls, and left a personal message for Mr. Jennings. Then I joined Phil upstairs, scarcely breathing for fear of disturbing his restless sleep. It helped neither of us that when daylight came it showed up Myron's possessions still standing around.

But somehow I rose clear-headed and full of new energy. Before all the arranging and questionings, I needed to make that hasty trip home to The Crescent.

Mr. Pearson offered himself as escort, Phil wanted to go with me, but I had to do this alone. The café was shut and I left the boys in Grandma's capable hands. It would be a help to her to have that absorbing task.

Before nine I caught a fast train. The now familiar journey didn't take long. And then, one first glimpse of the house told me instantly that my life here was at an end. There were too many abiding ghosts under this roof. If I could bear with them, it was too much to expect of Phil. The kindest plan was to put the old home straight on the market.

Well, I would do it! In a short while, when the first numbing shock of this tragedy lessened a little.

Briefly I saw Kay White — she had no idea what to say to me — and other neighbours, and left them my Brighton address. I checked a stream of phone messages and emails, answered some, noted others. Then I moved around the house filling bags and suitcases, ferrying them out to my car.

After that, one by one I shut the doors in the silent house, blotting out each room. The bedroom where Myron passed his last troubled night, the sitting room where Marla talked to me — the kitchen where Myron gave me the opal ring that had lived up to its fancied ill-omen. It glimmered now, pale and cold, on my cold hand.

Last of all I returned to the room we had made an office, with its memories of hours of work that promised such success. I remembered Stanhope Hill, all those crusades against injustice or incompetence.

From a stray leaflet Myron's bright dark eyes looked up straight into mine. Then I sat down at the table and bowed my head down on it, and long-delayed tears came in a great flood. I wept for the pity of it, for the cruel waste. Maybe, indeed, I had married a mirage — but there were many shared moments we had known that I would treasure for always. When the recollection of those unhappy fights and quarrels had dimmed, still his voice and his face would never leave me, the sound of him laughing in the sunshine.

I rose and shut the office door, and walked out of the house. In the loaded car I set off to drive quietly and steadily towards the coast. Back to the shining sea, to the summer time people still absorbed in their own world.

A paper-seller's placard, *Two Die in Hotel Horror*, would be for them just a momentary pause, a passing pang of sympathy.

★ ★ ★

Inevitably the tragedy would be much publicised. All Myron could have wanted for his 'public image' was accorded him now. So far as I could, I kept out of it. There were many onlookers ready to describe what they had seen.

Also, of course, the whole affair had to be investigated — and it was my one longing that the underlying dark truths could stay hidden, so all the honour accorded to Myron might stay unsullied. And mercifully, my prayer was answered: a half-told story, a compassionate silence, sufficed. Marla's moods and behaviour had caused concern of late to people who knew her, quite naturally traced back to the death of her baby in appalling circumstances never yet cleared up. She had cut herself off from her sparse family and confided in no one. So a simple explanation for her last act was ready to hand: she was upset because Myron had married someone else, she had a morbid obsession concerning small boys, she was trying to break up his and my life together. She wasn't really responsible for her actions.

There was even a ready explanation

for Myron's intention to visit the police station on that fateful day, his anxiety about her veiled threats to Phil and Richie. It was all true, every word. Everything fitted in. What remained unsaid was the secret of just the few of us closest to him — and if we did wrong to withhold it, I had no regrets.

His last public performance was highly esteemed. No one mentioned any more the petty dishonesty that had caused such shocked embarrassment. The management at Hanley's — and Old Jennings personally — sent flowers for him.

Back in London, I found the tributes and sympathy were overwhelming. Myron knew so many people. The simplest words, like the shaky note from old Mrs. Chivers, were the most moving to me. But the day of the funeral passed, the most beautiful flowers withered, the last letter was answered — and somehow the days went by, life was going on.

John Challoner was back at Hanley's.

Sophie was caring for her family of pets. The Pearsons — I rang them twice daily — were coping with the late-season trade as summer waned fast to early autumn chills. Evie Gillespie had put the last item into her album of Myron's press cuttings. For me, the time was coming to move on.

Malcolm Fraser, my brother-in-law, had journeyed to London for the funeral: regretfully alone, because Jan was having problems and the occasion might be too stressful for her. He suggested I might care to stay with his family a while: especially because, with Jan's baby due almost any day, it might help me to have the task of assisting her and caring for the other children. I remembered the kindness of the Fraser family at the time of the rail accident. I yearned now for Janine's loving companionship.

All the luggage we might need was packed. The house in The Crescent was left to its silence and its ghosts. I was still determined to sell the place.

But I would stay with Jan at least until her baby was born: I was too weary to plan far beyond that.

On the day I left with the boys for Scotland, John came to the station to see us off. Really I had scarcely seen him since the day Myron died. He was present at the funeral, of course. He rang a few times offering any help I needed, he wrote a couple of sympathetic, very remote letters. That was all. I didn't know if I had expected more.

Already he had told me he never anticipated marrying again — and I did undeniably turn him down point blank when Myron tried almost to force us together. The very fact of Myron doing that seemed to have driven us apart. We would never be able to blot out so many painful scenes from our minds. More than that, I wasn't sure I wanted an emotional involvement ever again. I longed only for peace.

'I don't know how long we'll be staying,' I told John at the station. 'A few weeks; anyway. It won't hurt Phil to miss a little school, he's not sleeping or eating properly — he's not at all himself.'

John said, 'I see. Is it likely to become a permanent arrangement?'

'To end up getting myself a house near the family? It would be nice for all of us.'

He stood beside me, tall and grave and unsmiling. I wondered how it had once been so easy to talk to him. I had to force myself to ask, 'How about your plans?'

'I'm still definite about a new start. My sister rang me again yesterday . . . '

I nodded. There was no point in asking how far his arrangements had progressed. They were going ahead, and that was enough to know.

He said suddenly, with clear embarrassment, 'There's something I wanted to say to you, Thelma. But — it's not very easy.'

I met his eyes and read their concern for me, their distaste for whatever he was trying to say. Really, he had already made it plain enough. I suggested, 'Just write it, if you feel you must. But you don't have to. Now I must get the boys settled down . . .'

They were close beside me, Phil getting agitated in case the train left without us. John answered me abruptly, 'It just seems rather cowardly to put it in a letter.'

'I think we've been through too much to worry how things seem.' I managed a wavery smile. 'I hope things work out for you. Give our love to Sophie, she's a lovely girl and — I'll miss her . . . Goodbye.'

'Goodbye,' he echoed.

I wondered whether I should ever see him again. I wondered too, wearily, whether it really mattered.

The long journey with the children was the nightmare I had anticipated. Despite the smoothly speeding wheels, it seemed to take an eternity. Richie was his ever-demanding self, and even the amenable Phil ignored the books and games I had brought with us. But when at last the train pulled into the big, busy terminus, it was a great relief to find Malcolm waiting for us — and his welcome gave me a sudden sense of coming home. My sister was a little better, he said, but under strict orders to rest. And she was longing to see me.

The longing was mutual. Somehow the final part of the journey was got through; with Richie now heavily asleep. He woke more crotchety than ever when Malcolm's car pulled up at the familiar house. I saw Phil gazing at the scene wistfully — of course picturing our last time here, when Myron was with us.

'Thelma!' The front door opened and Jan came rushing out, half laughing and half crying, with arms held out to me. She clasped me close, struggling for words. 'It's so *wonderful* to see you . . . oh, I did so want to come to you, and they wouldn't let me . . . oh, I'm so very, very sorry . . . '

It was Malcolm who firmly detached her and insisted we all go inside. In a confused bunch we went into the pleasant room I remembered, the window overlooking the green garden. Bright-faced Kirsty sidled up to say 'hello'.

But none of that really registered with me. I was looking at the shining-new pram with a soft pink cover. I whispered, 'Phil — Richie — come and see! But be very quiet . . .'

My prosaic Barrington heart gave a great thrust of pain and joy and thanksgiving as I studied the tiny face of Lucie Marina, Lesley's longed for little girl, with already an immature image of her mother's sprite-like prettiness. For a moment I could say nothing. Richie announced to all and sundry, 'Baby!'

'That's right, sweetheart.' Jan encouraged Phil, still hanging back, to come nearer. 'She's your little sister, Phil, yours and Richie's. She's safe home from the hospital. Your Mummy and Dad left her for all of us to care for.'

Still I couldn't trust my voice, but Phil seemed not to want words. I saw his tense face relax into the first real smile that had lighted it for many days. For a little boy who had known so much loss, it was wondrous delight to experience gain instead.

The Fraser parents came through from the kitchen with lavish trays of refreshments, and greeted us all very kindly. We sat around, and talked of harmless things. It was an indescribable comfort just to be part of a family group.

A while later, when the children had been extinguished in their various beds — Richie by now worn out, Phil still in a dreamy haze — I had some time alone with Jan. The Fraser parents had left. Malcolm was clearing up the kitchen.

Jan was flopped wearily in a low armchair with her feet on a stool. But she began to chatter very eagerly.

'Thelma, now listen to me! You're *not* going back to that house where so many bad things happened! We *all* want you to come here to live! . . . '

'Please!' I stemmed the tide of words. 'It's a lovely thought, but — I do need a little time before — '

'Oh, of course, you can't rush things. It was all so dreadful, I cried and cried . . . we didn't know your Myron very well but we all liked him so much . . . '

'Well. That's how it was. Most people did.'

'And he was so clever, and so brave, and so young . . . Would you rather not talk about it? Or does it help?'

'I don't think I can talk about it now. Perhaps another time.'

She was a loving and sympathising soul. She had always seemed closer to Lesley than to me — but now there were only the two of us left of the original Barrington family from The Crescent. It was a precious bond between us.

And what was there — today, or all the tomorrows — to tie me still to the old home?

Just a few hours at the Fraser home made me aware their object was to give me a rest and a holiday, in spite of Malcolm's hints about 'helping out'. But I decided just as quickly I wasn't to be coddled. Very soon I started taking over various chores — and especially caring for the children to keep the house quiet for Jan.

Richie was quickly back to his busy, sticky, time-consuming self. His little cousin Kirsty had taken a great liking to him, so they were inseparable. But Phil seemed to find the greatest happiness in helping me wheel his baby sister along to the seafront on many afternoons. He walked beside me, holding on to the Frasers' double-buggy (for Richie in sit-up-and-fidget mode and Lucie in lie-back-and-doze) and watching the small face that so vividly reflected his mother's. He soon tired of building teetering sandcastles with the little ones, and returned to sit beside me, his hand still protectively touching the pram.

The breeze lifted his dark hair, brought a healthier colour to the thin little face already losing its shadows. It was pure joy to me.

He said wistfully, on one of those outings, 'When we're back home, I won't ever get to see Lucie. Will I?'

'We might not go home for long. Would you like to live somewhere near here?'

'Here? Could we really? Oh, but there's school . . . '

'They have schools here too.' I smiled at his eagerness. If Phil could be made happy by these surroundings and the tiny clinging hands of Lucie, was that not the only answer?

And I hoped and prayed that this group of growing, needing, loving children would fill for me a future that never, it seemed now, would be wholly complete. For the promised letter from John was merely a few stilted lines, hoping we were well, offering any help he could give. And Sophie wished to send her love. That was all.

Reading between those remote lines, the truth was obvious. His delicacy of feeling, after the supreme tragedy we had shared, held him far aloof. Perhaps, like me, he drew back on the brink of more emotional involvement in his life. Perhaps he had simply thought better of it, wondering whether he really wanted to share his future with the grieving widow and family of someone he had known well, had seen die. Maybe it was better so.

But for a few days, those thoughts were totally eclipsed from my mind. Jan was hurried to the hospital, and her son was safely born. Malcolm, who had very much wanted a boy, went about in a state of delight and confusion both touching and comical.

Late on the next Saturday morning, following a hectic round of chores and shops, I set off again with the children to our favourite stretch of beach. It was a golden day but held a distinctly crisp hint of autumn. I tucked a fleecy cover more closely around Lucie, positioning the pram away from the breeze. Phil, with bare sandy feet, sat beside me. Kirsty and Richie grubbed together with plastic spades, squabbling amiably over pebbles and shells.

When a voice beside me spoke my name, I didn't turn immediately. There were times, especially in those long nights when sleep wouldn't come and I missed Myron so much, that often I seemed to hear voices. Malcolm and his parents were all by now at the hospital with Jan — so who else would speak my name? . . .

'Thelma?' this voice said again. 'They said when I rang a little time ago that you'd be somewhere along here.'

This time it was no delusion of sorrow and loneliness. Phil, screwing his head round, exclaimed in wonder, 'Look, Auntie! — it's Uncle John! — look!'

'Look!' John Challoner repeated. 'So it is.'

I turned to him, the tall figure topped by dark silvered hair, the thoughtful eyes, the smile slow and hesitant. In a manner not entirely welcoming I mumbled, 'Oh, it's you!'

Phil couldn't wait to announce eagerly, 'This is my new sister. She's called Lucie.'

'Of course, your sister.' John bent to look at her. 'She's lovely, Phil. You and Richie must be very proud of her.'

'Richie isn't very. He likes Kirsty better, she can play with him.'

John followed his gaze to the two young children nearby. 'Thelma, are you understudying the Old Woman Who Lived in a Shoe?'

I laughed politely. There would be one more to add to the group, I said, when my sister's newborn son James left the hospital. He asked how everyone was, and I enquired after Sophie, who was staying the weekend with a neighbour. He told me he had visited the Pearsons, who had settled down very well considering. They had, I agreed, I rang them regularly and I believed they were possibly retiring to a house along the coast to do a few 'b & b's', less wearing than the long-standing rigours of the café.

All those formal words, words, words, seemed almost meaningless. After a few minutes of them my inborn bluntness had to ask, 'What made you come all this way?'

'To see you. To talk to you.'

'You wrote to me. I thought — ' I stopped there and told Phil to join the other children for a while — 'Just keep them busy a few minutes!' I huddled Lucie's covering a little more closely around her. 'John, what I'm trying to say — you didn't need to trail up here. The letter was enough. You don't have to explain . . . '

He had lowered his tall presence down beside me, sitting awkwardly bolt-upright. He was frowning, as ill at ease as I was. The look of him, the nearness of him, sent my mind rushing back to memories I would rather forget.

'I've been in quite a quandary,' he was saying, not answering me. 'I've tried to phone you, I've tried to put it in writing. You've a right to know. But — I just didn't know how to do it — '

'To do what? You're talking in riddles.'

'Well. Here goes, then.' He took an envelope from an inner pocket and laid it in my lap. 'You should have this, if anyone should. But it's going to be quite a shock to you . . . '

There had been shocks and to spare during these past months. I opened the envelope and the first of its contents slipped out: a folded and crumpled cutting from a newspaper.

'You might not remember — you probably didn't even notice,' John's voice was going on, 'but that day — when Marla fell — she had a handbag on a shoulder strap. It came open, everything was scattered about . . . '

I had seen already a heavy black headline: '*THIS IS MURDER!* — *There is no other name for the death of tiny*

Richard Dalston, caused by the reckless motorist who left him dying at the roadside . . . ' The print blurred before my eyes, but the last few words in accusing capitals stood out: *'THIS CALLOUS KILLER MUST BE BROUGHT TO JUSTICE! — WHO IS THIS FIEND ON WHEELS?'* Beneath, in a cramped handwriting I knew, was written *'Ask Myron Gillespie.'*

I exclaimed with a shudder of revulsion, 'That's horrible!'

'There are others, all similar, all with the same sort of comments. Don't read them unless you want to.'

'I don't want to! But I don't see how — '

'I picked up the envelope. When I saw what was inside I didn't hand it in with the rest of the poor girl's belongings. I kept it. Ever since, locked in a drawer.'

Silently I looked at him, with dawning realisation that my hands held a damning accusation that would blacken Myron's name for ever in the eyes of the world, whether it could be proved now or not. But for John's action the sordid story would have blazed into the open. Myron had lived day by day with consuming guilt, and finally had paid with his life. Did he indeed deserve this epitaph?

'I had no right to do it,' John was saying. 'At the time it seemed the only thing to do. But — there's something else beside the paper cuttings, you'd better look at that too. Especially at that.' He took the envelope from me and extracted a small colour photograph. 'I'm so sorry. I'm doing this very badly.'

I looked at the photo. Fresh from the perfection of Lucie I saw another baby, with wide open eyes strangely dull, with an almost wizened little face. Around the head on its white pillow showed up hair strangely long and thick — and flaming, glowing red.

'Then it *was* his child! He swore to me it wasn't. He swore to me!'

If Myron indeed had turned in

repugnance from this tiny pitiful Richard and his mother, perhaps indeed there were more grounds than we knew for Marla's state of mind?

'It's not proof, of course,' John was saying. 'Coincidences do happen. You could probably find out the truth if you want to.'

'I don't want to. I don't think I want to know.'

I was still gazing at the pictured face. John's voice seemed to come from a vast space.

'That's what I thought. I couldn't let it all be made public — and yet I couldn't hide this away and forget I ever found it. So I had to see you, to tell you. And now it's done I can start getting my own affairs straightened out . . . '

Of course, I thought, bleakly, he had a lot of arrangements to make for a move across the globe. I faltered, 'Then — Sophie is really having the big change you spoke about.'

'That's right. I'm not too old for a

new venture. Not quite.'

My hands fumbled with the envelope in my lap. I saw it now through a blur. I had thought it didn't matter where John went, what he chose to do. But it did matter.

'You like living here, don't you?' he was saying.

I nodded. I couldn't look at him, but I thought there was a glimmer of a smile lighting his serious face.

'I thought so. You know, I never did give my sister a definite decision. It's a long, long way . . . and Sophie couldn't take her beloved pets! But she could take them somewhere rather nearer. Thelma, I'd heard some rumours at Hanley's, and last week I bearded Old Jennings in his den. He's not really a bad old buffer. He confirmed there'll be a new branch office opening in Scotland — a whole new project — possibly late next year, certainly the year after. He was quite happy to put my name forward for the managership — with a strong recommendation, he said. It's likely to be well within reach of this area. So — ?'

A moment ago all had been emptiness. I whispered, 'You'd really change all your plans? So — we could still — ?'

'We could still work out our future together. We can look for a house with a nice garden for the boys . . . if you want that as much as I do. When you're ready.'

I wasn't ready yet. But there was plenty of time. There was the rest of our lives.

I looked across the sandy beach at Phil, busily filling up a plastic bucket for Kirsty while Richie admired their very lopsided castle. Then I looked again at the miserable little bundle of papers.

'I'll burn these cuttings when I get back to the house. Every one of them. But — ' The little photograph was still in my hand. 'Please,' I said softly, 'will you watch the children for me just for a moment?'

Down to the water's edge I walked

alone, where the retreating sea had left a spread of shining clean-washed sand bright in the sunshine. I stepped on a little further right into the ebbing water. I touched my lips to the pictured face before I laid it down with gentle reverence. And the retreating tide received it, and bore it quietly, tenderly away.

So find your rest, tiny Richard who scarcely knew life. So gain peace, lonely grieving mother, from your sickness and your wrongs. And so sleep, like son of like father, young wasted life from wasted life — my brilliant, restless Myron of the ready tears, of the unforgettable smile. A man so blessed and so cursed. A man so greatly gifted and so grievously flawed . . .

No one who had known him would forget him. For me his presence would live on eternally. So now he was with me on the sparkling seashore. But this was no sunburst, only the lingering gold of a year already fading, a summer almost spent.

As I went slowly back to the little group along the beach, fighting back the tears that filled my eyes, I saw John waiting for me. A warm sustaining hand reached for mine. His voice whispered close beside me, 'Amen.'

Between the two of us there were needed no more words.

THE END

We do hope that you have enjoyed reading this large print book.

Did you know that all of our titles are available for purchase?

We publish a wide range of high quality large print books including:
Romances, Mysteries, Classics
General Fiction
Non Fiction and Westerns

Special interest titles available in large print are:
The Little Oxford Dictionary
Music Book, Song Book
Hymn Book, Service Book

Also available from us courtesy of Oxford University Press:
Young Readers' Dictionary
(large print edition)
Young Readers' Thesaurus
(large print edition)

For further information or a free brochure, please contact us at:
Ulverscroft Large Print Books Ltd.,
The Green, Bradgate Road, Anstey,
Leicester, LE7 7FU, England.
Tel: (00 44) **0116 236 4325**
Fax: (00 44) **0116 234 0205**

SPADES AND HEARTS

Wendy Kremer

When Sara takes over her aunt's market garden in a small country village, she becomes a part of village life and loses her heart to James, a customer. James initially doubts her capabilities, but finds he's not just interested in the vegetables from her garden . . . Meanwhile, there is Ken, an old rival of James, and there's also Pamela, James' attractive assistant who wants to be more. Love grows and flourishes. Who will harvest, and who'll be left empty-handed?

DISCOVERING ELLIE

Valerie Holmes

Ellie lives a sheltered life under the guardianship of her Aunt Gertrude. Despite living with the shadow cast over her mother's respectability — commonly said to have run off with a French lover; deserting her only child — Gertrude has raised her niece alongside her own daughters, Esme and Cybil. However, when the handsome Mr Gerald Cookson returns to the old hall he reveals to Ellie the truth behind her past, and discovers a very different future for them both.